Judy Lee-Fenton has written for magazines, newspapers, factual articles, short story fiction and has written two factual books. This is her first fiction book. She is a Tai Chi instructor, chair of the Essex Tai Chi Academy. A member of the Theosophical Society and has spent several years with a spiritual teacher. Judy has a lifetime interest in all things esoteric. She has three children from her first husband and nine grandchildren. With her third husband she spent several years sailing around the Mediterranean and has sailed many other seas. Judy presently lives in Maldon, Essex.

My daughter Nicola and sons Adrian and Julian, who are just amazing.

Judy Lee-Fenton

RAW AWAKENINGS

AUSTIN MACAULEY PUBLISHERS™

LONDON • CAMBRIDGE • NEW YORK • SHARJAH

A CIP catalogue record for this title is available from the British
Library.

ISBN 9781398405516 (Paperback)
ISBN 9781398405523 (ePub e-book)

www.austinmacauley.com

First Published (2021)
Austin Macauley Publishers Ltd
25 Canada Square
Canary Wharf
London
E14 5LQ

Chapter 1

"Oh my," Jacelet said to herself. She peered over the edge with controlled care, looking down into the deep violet depths.

"That's scary."

She took a deep steadying breath. This was her time of day; she owned the sunset. These untamed mountains, the setting sun, the tumbling of red fingers spreading down the snowy slopes, and as she watched the sun depart, new steel blue edges joined the red fingers. It was all hers. With another deep breath, she filled her very being with all the wild beauty. Then with such a feeling of contentment, she slowly spread her large blue/black wings and with the last of the sun shimmering on her feathers, reflecting a myriad of colours. Jacelet leant forward and let the thermals lift her up. She glided across the valley, back up to the mountains, turning sharply, she felt the spray of the waterfall across her right side as it thundered majestically down the rocks racing down to join the river at the bottom of the valley. Another deep breath, and a slight tilt. The downdraft took her within seconds and she soared down to the valley floor, twisting last minute with the edges of her great wings brushing the water. Then, zooming up, at a dangerous angle. What power, dicing against death and injury. Jacelet soared as high as she could.

Just one more dive, she thought, *then I will go.* It was her greatest passion, flying. Nothing gave her such exhilaration, freedom and wonderment.

Bliss, she thought, *Maybe as good as bedding Zude?* The idea made her laugh and then shudder, as she imagined his fingers running down her body.

"Almost." And laughing and gave herself up to flight.

Chapter 2

Far across the valley, Flute watched Jacelet with mixed feelings – admiration for the way she flew, jealous of the beauty that enchants Zude. Anger that she was put in this position. Life for both Jacelet and Flute would be perfect if it wasn't for the other.

Neither of them wanted to share Zude.

Elsewhere, Zude lifted his head, disturbed from his meditations, and felt the vibrations in the air. From Flute – discord, and Jacelet – ecstasy. With a twisted smile, he returned to his thoughts.

Flute spread her wings, she must return before she was missed. She really didn't want Zude to know she had been watching Jacelet. Soaring high, she flew away from the sun, away from Jacelet's world towards her own, that she ruled with Zude. Her white feathers spreading to catch the wind. Pleasure spreading through her body, as she journeyed home. Flute loved the flight, and with every change of breeze, she dived, turned and rolled, embracing the changes, even though it lengthened the journey, putting herself at risk. She couldn't resist the thrills.

Jacelet was also turning for home, it would soon be dark and she had a council meeting. She knew she might be late, so flew direct. It would be another 14 or 15 sunsets before Zude would be back until then she had the responsibility of the Protacths Race.

She landed and turned to view the mountains one more time. Sudden flashes and odd changes of colour, far away in the distant sky caught her attention.

She had never seen a sky like that before, that was really weird, she must tell Zude.

Zude was in council with the Elders and the discussion was fast and furious. The Elders stated categorically that it was time for the Protacths and Biacts to progress more to mind usage and on that point, the wings had to go. Zude protested that it was too soon, some were not ready for such a move. It would cause great trouble.

He thought of his two Queens, how much they loved flying and how they would struggle to adjust and of course, they had to lead by example. Well, he had to start with Flute; he was with her for the next 15 sunsets.

Jacelet hurried into the gathering. A few easy problems that she delegated to her councillors and she was done. Easier to solve then Zude's council she thought.

Things were changing, she too could feel the vibes, but was aware her probing was blocked when she related her mind into the Elders.

Flute was watching the night sky turn from red to purple. She was unsettled, feeling change in the air, but unable to source them. She turned carefully, her large wings folded back, she smoothed her feathers lovingly. With her ice-blue eyes, glanced once more at the distant sky. Something caught her attention; there it was again, dark flashes and strange colours; disturbed, she turned. Zude will be back soon and then she will demand to know everything.

It can't be true, travel by mind; the wings will have to go! It wasn't right. Zude stood his ground while Flute raved and thrashed around, as much as her large wings would allow. She railed against Zude, saying he must change the law, see the Elders and tell them it can't be. She pounded her fists on his chest until she was exhausted. Zude stood his ground and watched and waited. Finally spent, she flung herself on the ground and sobbed. Vowing to herself, that she would not lose her wings.

The day of the Biacts gathering arrived. Heralded in by trumpets and panache. Zude took the stage and gave out the Elders' mandate. Standing tall, he concentrated his mind onto his magnificent white wings and to gasps of amazement and horror, he burnt them off. A few moments later, shocked, the Biacts followed Zude's lead. Only Flute remained to follow, but instead, she announced to all that she was keeping her wings. With controlled fury and disgust, an enraged Zude turned, directing his mind, burnt off her wings in front of all the Biacts. With uncontrolled rage, Flute screamed and launched herself at Zude. Flooring him, she landed heavily on top, hitting and spitting. Surrounded by the smell of burnt feathers, she unleashed a tirade of hate and abuse. Climaxing with, "Never will I forgive you."

Horrified and greatly saddened, Zude decided to go to the Protacths world sooner than he had planned. First he sat with his council, explaining how they had to practise and perfect travelling by mind control and then he issued his orders to Xen, his next in command. To keep an eye on the distant sky, as something odd was happening. Then left strict instructions that Flute was to be held in isolation until his return. Then, taking the form of the Protacths, he took off; his last flight in that form to be with his other Queen.

Jacelet nervously stood near the cliff edge, eagerly watching the sky for the first signs of Zude. She knew what to expect, for all the details of Flutes disgrace and humiliation had reached them all. She felt only sadness for Flute, being able to relate to her situation, for she knew that they were so alike in many ways. Jacelet was very uneasy, like Flute, she didn't want to lose her wings.

Zude flew in, folded his blue/black wings for the very last time and with relief took Jacelet into his arms. They took solace in each other. Later that night, Zude, after his sexual passion had been sated, comfortable beside Jacelet, running his fingers through her soft feathers and caressing her body, he finally began to talk. He revealed how much Flute had wounded and upset him. He felt humiliated by her behaviour. She was, after all, Queen of the Biacts and should have been an example to them all.

The next day Zude called all the Protacths to a gathering. This time with little ceremony, he related to them all what the Elders had proclaimed. Then, standing before them he burnt off his Protacths wings.

The Proteacths, well prepared, as one, followed their King's lead and soon all wings were destroyed.

Jacelet then proudly turned to Zude, with a look of love and with tears in her eyes, burnt off her wings. In the end, her love for Zude far outweighed her love of flying.

After yesterday, and the last night, the last thing she wanted to do was to cause any more sorrow for Zude. Also,

Jacelet was excited, eager and ready to embark on the next stage of the journey.

Zude was being summoned to the Elder's Council. He knew what to expect from them.

The laws of the universe were quite strict but just. Still, all the same, it was going to be a difficult task. He had spent a great deal of time thinking over the events with Flute and he had settled in his mind what he wished.

Zude stood in the centre of the sacred ring in the Protacths Hall and concentrated his thoughts, and moments later, he was standing in the Hall of Endeavour. He stood a moment and his form changed from Protacths to his true self. Two of the Elders stepped forward to greet him and although they were tall, Zude stood well above them.

No need for words, for thoughts passed rapidly between them.

Entering the huge Hall of Justice, the three of them strolled on the marble floors through huge pillars that seemed to disappear into the vastness above. By each pillar stood a sentinel guard, they too, were very tall and not so pretty in appearance.

Zude nodded his acquaintance to those he knew well and finally came to his place amongst others of his level. He looked around at the many forms and shapes that were attending. His eyes rested on his close friends, Mosstle and Reed. They were cosmic partners. Reed was particularly beautiful, with lovely long red hair and green eyes, but Mosstle in comparison, even with the same red hair and green eyes, was very craggy.

They came from a world of water and stone. Zude often visited them in their world. The horns sounded and all attention turned to the Wise One, standing head and shoulders above all others, his long white hair sweeping the ground seemingly intermingled with his gown. It had begun.

It was a hard two days. Although the Elders wanted Flute removed, Zude defended her saying he was sure that she would become better. It was a long and hard discussion and the vote was only just in Zude's favour. Any imbalance within the races was considered very serious.

But the biggest worry of all was the reports from the other side of the universe, of instability and it was spreading fast, causing an imbalance. Zude reported what his two Queens had seen. A surprising number of the council thought it was overrated and the vote was to wait and see. Zude and a number like him were extremely concerned.

They all planned to keep their own watch over the situation. Zude had his opinion that it was all much more dangerous than it had been acknowledged to them all, and he vowed to exchange thoughts with his close council companions of his own level.

Chapter 3

Jacelet paced up and down, turning and looking at the sacred ring. Knowing how silly all this was, it wouldn't make Zude come any quicker, but it had been three days now and he was never away at the Elder's council that long. She was nervous having just left her council, discussing mind flight; already several of the council were regretting the burning of the wings. Jacelet missed her wings more than she could say, but kept this to herself as she would always back Zude. Again, she wondered, how well did she know Zude. Having always thought that Flute and herself were the only two Queens. Today, messages had arrived for Zude that the Utech race had perfected their mind travelling and wanted to know which Kingdom they should travel too.

Should the council bring their Queen first? Who were the Utechs and why would they want to travel to be with us?

Elsewhere, Flute was so restless in her isolation, every day getting angrier at Zude, then the council and finally, she bitterly started to lay the blame at Jacelet's feet.

It was her that bewitched Zude. He should be with her now, how dare he be with Jacelet. In her isolation, Flute began to plan.

Zude arrived back through the sacred ring still in the form of his true self. Although Jacelet didn't recognise the form, she knew instantly it was Zude. He had no feathers on his face, it was just bare skin and as she looked, no feathers on his arms either. She watched in amazement, as he changed his form back to the Protacths. Zude stepped out of the ring and meet Jacelet's gaze.

"You were not meant to see that," Zude held his arms out to Jacelet, "I didn't think you were ready yet." He embraced Jacelet with fierceness and love.

"You were so tall and bare."

Zude studied her face.

"Remember always, that the love I have for you is yours and yours alone."

"And Flute's."

"That is hers and hers alone, neither deflects from one, or the other. Do you understand Jacelet?"

"And the Utechs?" blurted Jacelet.

"Ahh, I see a lot has been happening while I was gone. Just remember what I said. We have difficult times ahead and I need you strong, I need you all strong."

And Zude began to explain about the Utechs and his Queen, Anka.

Later that day, when they all sat to take refreshment, Zude outlined what had been said by the Elders. How they wanted Flute replaced, how he had gone out on a limb to keep her and adding, he hoped that in her isolation, it had made her think clearer. He told of the friends he had met, of the fear of the unbalance in the far-off part of the universe. How many of the Elders did not think it was a threat and were complacent, but how he was very worried. How important it was that they all perfected mind travel. Jacelet looked over to those that had been grumbling and was gratified to see remorse and embarrassment on their faces. Zude went on to tell them about the third race, where Zude was also the King of the Utech's and of another Queen, they all knew nothing about. Zude thought it was very important that the three races came together to form one strong one. There was complete and utter silence for all these revelations.

Zude said, "A lot for you all to think about, think well."

Well, thought Jacelet, *they think they have a lot to think about, but I know more and have a strong feeling that there is a lot more to know about Zude, much more to come.*

She left with Zude feeling a strange mix of excitement and apprehension. Jacelet got little rest that night as Zude was unrelenting with his lovemaking, with a stronger passion then Jacelet had ever experienced, all on a new level.

"You now know me better than the other two and you are stronger for that," said Zude as he buried his head in the soft feathers of her stomach. "Remember that."

Next morning, Zude stood in the sacred ring and seconds later appeared in the Biacts world. He took the form of the Biacts and stepped out to be greeted by his Biact council. After refreshments, he was bought up to date with the progress of mind travel.

Zude then told them what he had told the Protacths the day before.

He left them to ponder over all news while he went to see Flute, knowing what he had to tell her about the Utech's was dicey when Flute was unstable. Their meeting was emotional and sexual, for what had happened had not touched the feeling between them. Although Zude was saddened by her

17

behaviour, he was sure she would change. Though secretly, Flute felt that she would never forgive Zude for the humiliation of burning off her wings. She still wanted Zude for herself, so putting the blame of it all on Jacelet's shoulders, she only half heard what Zude was telling her. Flute kept her plans closed in her mind not wanting Zude to zone in on her thoughts.

Zude was surprised that Flute had taken all the news quite well. With another Queen to deal with, he was expecting fireworks – he knew she could barely deal with the thought of Jacelet. Puzzled, he looked well at Flute and realised she possibly hadn't processed the information, her mind was elsewhere.

What was she up to now? thought Zude. Swinging his arm around her shoulders, they walked back together to the Halls.

Elsewhere, Jacelet was wondering how Flute had dealt with the thought of another Queen. Someone else to share Zude with. It was hard enough when it was just Flute and herself, knowing that Zude always kept the two races apart to minimise trouble, now he wanted three races to come together – how was that going to work? This would be a big test and on top of it all, more important by far, the disturbances in the balance of their universe. Jacelet laughed to herself, knowing which problem Flute would think the most important.

Jacelet and her council were summoned by Zude to come to the Biacts World. Thirteen of them stepped nervously into the sacred ring. Firstly, because it was so new to them travelling by mind, and secondly, wondering at their summons. Zude and Flute were there to greet them.

"You all made it then," laughed Zude, "no casualties." He strode forwards and shook hands with each councillor then turned, greeting Jacelet with a warm embrace. Jacelet felt Flute flinch, and their eyes met. Flutes smouldered.

Lord, how was this going to work? thought Jacelet.

"Council meeting of the three races first thing tomorrow morning."

Zude then held his hands out to his two queens, "Come."

"Three Races? What three Races?" Questioned Flute.

"Didn't you listen to anything I was saying yesterday?"

"What three races?" Demanded Flute.

Zude sighed and started again on the explanation of his three races and his three queens.

"I am your first Queen and why am I not enough?"

"All three of you have been there in different forms since time began, it is time you worked together."

"I am you first Queen," screamed Flute, "I won't have it."

"Whether you will have it or not, it is so, and Anka, with her council, will arrive later. Unlike you, they have lived without wings for some time, and you should learn from them. They are a logical race and we need them for balance."

Flute stormed off and Zude extended his hand to Jacelet. "Come."

She went with him, totally understanding Flute and how she felt, that alone was helping her accept the new Queen, not easily, but with a slow understanding.

Anka was beautiful, soft gold feathers shot through with tans and browns and soft brown eyes that looked quite gentle – she emanated calmness. Jacelet stepped forward to kiss her on both cheeks liking her at once.

"You are most welcome."

Jacelet looked round for Flute, but she was nowhere to be seen.

This is her world, thought Jacelet, *she should be here to greet Anka.*

Anka replied, "It is I that is honoured to meet you. I have heard so much about you all."

Heavens, thought Jacelet, *she knew all about us.*

Later, just before the evening feast, Jacelet sought Flute out. She found her sitting on the edge of the meeting square. Sitting and staring at the mountains.

Aware suddenly of Jacelet, she spun around.

"I should be up there flying," she spat angrily. "It's your entire fault."

Taken aback, Jacelet snapped back, "Where were you? I had to greet Anka on my own. Zude will not like this."

"Zude will do as I say, he is mine." Flute pushed past Jacelet, slapping her hard.

Staggering, Jacelet grabbed Flute to keep her balance.

"I will tell Zude you hit me," Flute said viciously. "He will believe me."

Neither noticed the odd skyline, strange colours and whirls.

Elsewhere, Zude was meeting with the three councils. The Utech's told of strange happenings in the sky. Of energy and magnetic disturbances affecting their Kingdom.

They were glad to leave as it was becoming so unstable and it also affected there thought process. They believed they left just in time.

Zude was very worried. "It is far more advanced than anyone thought; it sounds as if a collapse is not far away. I am leaving for the Elder's immediately."

Chapter 4

The bustle and volume of sound were the first things that struck Zude as he arrived at the Hall. Mosstle stepped forward to greet him.

"Thank God you have arrived. It's bad, and I don't want you or yours to get caught in the collapse. You should have all got out by now."

"Anka and her lot were moving straight here after I left, so there still is the Protacths and the Biacts to get out," Zude said as he and Mosstle moved rapidly towards the dias.

"I will help. First, report to the wise one, meanwhile I will organise some others to help.

"There has been such a panic since they realised it was collapsing. As you know the Elders never panic!!! Too much complacency." Mosstle angrily remarked.

Zude moved hastily, time was of the essence because here it was timeless and back there, in comparison, days will have passed. First, to consult the wise one.

Get them to concentrate on trying to hold; it might slow the collapse down, that might work for a short time, thought Zude.

He looked up and the wise one nodded. Zude knew he had picked his thought up and was agreeing.

Turning rapidly, he ran back to the entrance. Mosstle and the others were there, waiting.

"It is too dense in matter for any of us to make it through to your worlds. We will set up a vacuum bubble for your lot to enter into, but it will only last two days of your time before we have to withdraw the bubble. You have to make sure all of them make it by then.

"You will all have to crawl through the web to reach the entrance."

"Zude, wait."

He turned and saw that it was Danka, from the reptilian world.

"We can take a form that can cope with the denser matter and so are working out on how to be with you. Don't wait for us, go."

Zude dashed for the sacred ring. He was so relieved that the Protacths had been already moved to the Biacts World; at least they were in one place.

Chapter 5

Zude stepped out of the sacred ring into controlled havoc. Jacelet was organising the exodus of the two tribes, sending as many of the Protacths and Biacts that had established mind travel through the sacred ring.

"Great," said Zude, "Get as many out as you can before the link is gone."

He grabbed Jacelet and embraced her, kissing her on her black/blue feathered cheek and looking in her dark eyes whispered, "Love you. I'll find someone take over from you and then I want you with me. We are short of time. Now I must find Flute," with that Zude was gone.

Outside, he looked at the skyline. In the distance, it was black with great flashes of forked lightning, red-edged with black and whirling circles spitting out black energy while at the same time, sucking in what was surrounding. The atmosphere hung around him like a heavy cloak and it shook Zude to the core.

I have seen and dealt with bad situations, but this, he thought. He turned and ran into the citadel, he could see Flute ahead, standing with one of his commanders.

"Flute, come with me, and you, commander, take over from Jacelet at the sacred ring and send her to me here."

Zude winded his arms around Flute, kissed her white feathered cheek, looked into her ice-blue eyes.

"Love you and I want you to stick to my side, I need to know you are there."

Large explosions hit the air and knocked the pair off their feet. A black hole opened in the far distance, gaped and gulped, sucked in everything around it and disappeared. Zude rolled over to cover Flute and the both laid together, shocked for a moment, then galvanised into action. Running together made it into the citadel.

One of the Bicats' commanders approached Zude.

"The universe is getting smaller by the moment and will not withstand the outside pressures much longer. There is a wormhole opening and I would like to take as many as possible to try that way of escape, it gives a lot of us more chances, despite the dangers."

Zude agreed, the chances of sudden collapse and high radiation of a wormhole was probably marginally better than the total destruction of a collapsed universe.

Zude said, "Go."

Jacelet blew into the citadel covered with dust-like substance stammering out, "The sacred ring has gone, most of them have gotten out."

Zude looked at the stragglers making their way towards him.

"Over there," he shouted, "over there, join the commander, he is taking you through a wormhole. Hurry."

"What do we do now," Jacelet grabbed Zude's hand, "where do we go?"

"We have a way. Firstly, check who is left."

Zude started to look round when another massive explosion toppled the pillars holding up the grand archway into the citadel.

"We trapped," Flute screamed.

"Hold on," Zude checked how many were in the citadel. They were about 10 of them.

The bubble can just about hold that many, he thought.

"Right," he said, "listen to me. The Elders have set up a bubble on the edge of this level, to get there we have to use mind and travel the web. Stay close, everyone."

"Right, stand in a circle holding hands and concentrate, visualise the edge of the web."

Another large explosion caused dust and fragments to filter down onto the group.

"Don't break concentration," said Zude in a steady voice, "whatever you do, don't break the link."

With the collapse of the building around them, the group held their ground and suddenly, all of them were there at the edge of the web. A collective sigh escaped from them all.

"Don't break the mind link," warned Zude. "Going through the web is as much mind as it is physical. There are dangers in the web, don't let them distract you, it is very important that you hold the mind link."

They all stood at the edge of the web, it started vertical, but all knew it could change its direction at any given time.

"Use your bodies and mind together as a unit, and keep an eye on who is around you. The web changes as we go, the trick is to keep mind contact at all time. First foot on together and keep the mind links."

As they all stood on the web, it enlarged all the gaps and then immediately shrunk them again.

"Keep the mind contact," said Zude, this time his voice was in everyone's head. Second step, third step. The web moved lateral, then downhill.

"Keep the mind contact." Zude's voice echoed in each of their minds. "Let me hear your mind voices."

Zude was flooded with answers.

"Good."

Next step, the web uprighted itself and all of them suddenly appeared to be just hanging in space. One of them stumbled, "I can't do this."

"Yes you can, don't break the mind link."

Another step and another, the web seemed to be getting wet and slippery, everyone's hands were covered with goo.

"Hold your mind and think dry. Hold."

Another step and it became dry.

"Well done all, keep the mind link."

Darkness descended and no one could see anything. Zude's voice was in their minds.

"Steady, keep the link and see in your mind."

The web's next trick was to show in everyone's mind that they were still on the first step.

"Nooo, it can't be. My legs hurt."

"I can't do it."

"I'm so tired."

"It's an illusion," came Zude's mind voice.

"We are over halfway, keep strong."

Immediately, they were all back on the halfway rungs, but there was no further rungs going upwards.

Again, Zude's voice said, "Hold still, know that we are over halfway, but be on your guard."

Zude turned to check where Flute and Jacelet were climbing and was gratified to see they were climbing side by side.

"Up everyone, I think I can see the bubble." With renewed strength they faced the web, tackling it with a vengeance. The web began to spin.

"Oh no, I feel sick." Flute and Jacelet linked their arms with each other.

"Close your eyes it might help."

"I think that's worse," Jacelet replied.

Suddenly, they were all upside down.

"Hold on," said Zude, "I believe the bubble is edging down. When it reaches us you have to jump quickly into it and it will let you through. Hold on everyone, it's lowering; we must jump together."

"My foot has gotten twisted in the web," Jacelet said to Flute. "Can you see where it is caught?"

Flute stepped down one rung and gazed at Jacelet's foot.

"Keep moving it backwards and forwards and it come free. I will help, here," said Flute.

She looked up to see how near the bubble was and twisted a bit more over Jacelet's foot.

Zude cried, "Ready everyone, jump now."

All leapt in unison, passing through into the bubble.

"All here," checked Zude.

"All here," said Flute.

Zude sent a mind message to the Elders that all were aboard. The bubble shimmered and passed through to another level.

Zude turned to Flute and said, "That was too close." He then turned to speak to Jacelet.

"Where's Jacelet," he shouted, "where is she?"

Frantically, he looked around and realised that she had been left behind, to certain destruction.

Chapter 6

The bubble appeared with a squelch in the hall of the Sacred Ring and dissolved, leaving the occupants shaken and bewildered, but alright. As they stood up, the feathered bodies of the old universe dissolved away, leaving them standing in their true self bodies, each one of them looked at each other than at themselves – adjusting and astounded.

Mosstle raced forward and grabbed Zude, "Thank God you are okay, how is everyone else?"

"Jacelet's missing," said a frantic Zude, "she was there right to the last minute. Flute said she was right beside her when they all jumped."

Mosstle swung around to look at Flute, he scanned her face with a fierce and hard look.

"Come," he said to Zude, "let's gather the others, Danka is missing too, and she went in after you. Did you see her at all."

"No," replied Zude, his hands helplessly covered his face and then looked up at Mosstle with despair in his eyes.

Mosstle summoned a group to take care of the other occupants of the bubble. Then he, Zude and Flute set off to meet with the Elders to see what could be done.

"Perhaps they can halt or turn back the timing to see what happened to Jacelet," remarked Mosstle, as he glanced at Flutes facial expression.

The wise one turned to greet Zude. "Good news, it seems that Danka reached Jacelet at the point of collapse and enfolded her into her reptile body, then through a wormhole into Danka's world. We are aware that both were badly injured. Danka needs urgent welding, but I am sure that they are receiving good care. I know you will want to leave at once. You have our leave and blessings."

Zude sank to his knees and rocked backwards and forwards. Mosstle gently pulled him to his feet. "Bear up, bear up. I will come with you."

Flute added, "I will come as well."

"No way, you will stay here," Mosstle stated.

Zude looked from Flute's face to Mosstle's, wondering what was going on.

"Off you go," he said turning to Flute, "the council wants a word with you at once."

Flute turned.

"Zude, please," but Zude was already hurrying across the quadrangle with Mosstle in hot pursuit.

Dejected, she slowly walked towards the council hall.

I wonder if they know, she thought to herself. The answer was instantly in her mind. They know. She held her head high and jutted her chin as she defiantly walked into the Chamber. Behind her, the big double doors slammed shut.

Zude and Mosstle stood in the Scared Ring when Reed suddenly appeared.

"Just made it in time, I have only just heard about Jacelet and Danka." She reached and took Zude's hand in her own

30

and reached out with her other hand to Mosstle, her soul mate, saying, "Together we will make this alright."

And then, in a flash, they were gone from the Sacred Ring.

Chapter 7

It was such a dense and heavy atmosphere that it took a few moments for the threesome to adjust.

"Now I know why they have such heavy reptilian bodies." Reed stated, "Shall we take a reptilian body ourselves?"

"Let's stay as we are and see how it goes," said Zude, looking around in amazement.

"It's all so green."

There was steam coming off the ground as well as the water, and he felt how his body seemed to be steaming as well.

"Just see how it goes," he repeated.

A swish alerted them and waddling towards them was a reptilian Elder.

"Welcome, welcome," he hissed. "I find language difficult as it always comes out as a hiss," he said as he sucked back in his long narrow tongue.

"Don't let that put you off us, my name is Cracus, please come this way."

They waited till Cracus' long tail had moved off and then they followed.

"I wouldn't like to get in the way of that tail," whispered Reed to Mosstle, who chuckled and agreed.

"Everything is so big," said Zude, the vastness making his tall body feel small.

The reptilian Elders' hall astounded the trio, looking up they couldn't see the roof, green vegetation grew around the pillars of the grand hall and steam seemed to float everywhere. Large reptilian lay in the pools, hissing in their language to each other.

"I am feeling decidedly damp," Mosstle remarked. "Perhaps we should take a reptilian body after all."

Cracus hissed, "This way, this way." And he led the way through massive arches into a long hall that had a central platform that ran down the whole length of the hall.

On it stood various reptiles with wounds, gashes that were being welded by lasers that seemed to drop down from somewhere up in the high ceiling. The various colours were reflected in droplets and moisture in the hall, these kept dripping onto the trio, stinging and burning them.

Cracus urged them onto the platform and within moments the trio found their bodies covered with scales.

"That is for your protection while you are here. These reptilians are part of the force that helped remove Danka and Jacelet through the wormhole. They had to hold it open against the collapse of the universe while Danka brought Jacelet through."

Zude turned to Cracus and said, "Can you tell them all how much I am in their debt."

"No need to tell, they all know, they also know what work you do for the cosmos and you are held in high regard. We are also aware of the love Danka has for you, therefore, ours for yours."

"Where is Danka?" Zude asked,

"Come," said Cracus, and the trio stepped onto a moving walkway, which in moments delivered them to the far end of the hall. There on the platform lay Danka. Large angry-looking gashes were being welded together. Zude looked at the many ugly scars that already had been welded, tears came to his eyes and he thought himself onto the platform by Danka's massive head. Zude gently stroked her long nose and kissed her face under her eye. She opened her eyes to acknowledge Zude, snorted and fell back into unconsciousness.

"Thank you," Zude said gently, "thank you for your courage and your love and, of course, I do love you, Danka,"

She opened her eye again and snorted gently.

Mosstle and Reed were standing on the other side of Danka's massive face and were looking at the damage on that side. Mosstle looked up and realised that Zude hadn't seen it and shook his head at Reed in warning. They both said nothing and gave healing in their own manner as they stood there together. Finally, Cracus said, "We must leave her now to rest."

"Jacelet," said Zude.

"Jacelet now."

"I must explain to you all first how it was for Jacelet. When she missed the bubble, Danka was just behind her on the web. She found Jacelet barely conscious and tangled in the web. The only way for Danka to get her away was to take her into her own body. First, she held Jacelet in her mouth, while she fought her way to the wormhole, the universe was collapsing rapidly behind her so she had to fight against the vortex. At the entrance of the wormhole, her colleagues waited, holding off the negative energies that were swirling around. Danka had no choice but to swallow Jacelet, to protect her, knowing then that she had but a short time to get through the wormhole to save Jacelet. It was a horrendous journey with the wormhole collapsing behind them, some of the rear guard, I am sad to say, didn't make it. You saw the damage that the rest suffered. We tried to remove Jacelet by mind but it didn't work, so we lasered Danka open and removed Jacelet. Of course, her feathered body dissolved completely, but even her true self-body seems to have suffered acid burns. We conclude that her feathered body had started to dissolve inside Danka and that is why she is damaged. She now rests in a sealed pod with a suitable atmosphere around her, you can see her through the pod, but it will be a little while before consciousness returns."

Zude stood at the pod with his face and hands against the sides, studying Jacelet. She hung, suspended, while all the healing energies swirled around.

"She looks peaceful," he remarked to Mosstle, but how it hurt him not being able to enter and hold her. Together the trio stood holding hands and directed their concentrated thoughts for Jacelet's healing.

Jacelet's recovery was quite rapid thanks to all the healing she received. She was out of the pod and Zude was with her when she began to return to consciousness. Her eyes flickered open, bewildered.

"Where am I?"

"In Danka's world," said Zude, gathering his arms round Jacelet lifting her in a heartfelt embrace, it was so good to be holding her again.

"How did I get here?"

"I have been so worried. What do you remember?" said Zude gently.

Jacelet sighed, "We were on the web, my foot was caught in the webbing and Flute was trying to help me get free, but Zude she made it worse," whispered Jacelet her shoulders shaking as she sobbed.

Zude was remorseful, he didn't want to believe what Jacelet had said, but knowing Flute he knew it was a possibility; he held Jacelet until she fell asleep.

Zude sought out Mosstle, he confirmed what Jacelet had said.

"This is so serious. It will mean that Jacelet and Flute will have to have many lifetimes together to come to terms with each other and Flute will have to accept all the others in our group."

Mosstle gripped Zude's arm.

"You can have Reed as a logic balance on the lower levels and I will stay up here and work with the Elders."

"Where is Flute?"

"She is with the Elders, she was summoned as we left."

"Will you take Jacelet back with you, when you and Reed leave to see the Elders. I want to take a reptile body and spend some time with Danka. Of course, I will explain to Jacelet why; hopefully, she will more readily accept."

Zude's next visit to Jacelet was not going to be easy. She was still weak and a little emotional, but Zude knew she wanted to understand and grow with the knowledge.

He kissed her gently and then with more passion. He settled on the cushions with his arms around her and began to tell her about what had happened. How Danka had saved her, got her off the web, then the fought through the wormhole, the damage Danka and herself had suffered. How now the last universe no longer existed, their feathered bodies had gone and they were in there true self bodies. How, because of the discord between Flute and her, they would have to work it out between them in a series of lives on a lower level. Then Zude went on to say how that he was staying on in the reptile world with Danka, to have an experience of living with her and the reptile world.

"She is another of the first atoms. Like you, Flute and Anka. You all belong to me and each other."

Jacelet listened and absorbed. She accepted Danka as she had accepted Anka. She did so because of her love for Zude, also for her amazement of what Danka had done for her, understanding that it was Danka's love for Zude that ruled her too.

Chapter 8

Flute was pacing back and forth, she was mad as hell. Why should she put up with this treatment, after all, she was Zude's number 1 lady and here she was being treated as a criminal. All she did was a little bit of a twist with the web rope and look, no harm was done in the end. Just wait till Zude gets back, she will get him to change the ruling, after all, he wouldn't say no to her. Flute carried on pacing and grumbling.

The Elders were in deep debate. Zude had an important job to do in the Cosmos but he needed harmonious back up from his group, after all, he was only as strong as the weakest link and at this moment, that link was Flute. They would have to strengthen that link and strengthen the group's unity. After a great deal of discussion, it was decided to find a planet that could support life and set up a series of incarnations for the group to grow and become emotionally solid. Zude's group especially, need special training if they were to grow into unity, so it was recommended that they would retain no memory of who they were, except for Zude and his memory at this point would be partial. It was all decided. It became Law.

By the time Reed, Mosstle and Jacelet returned, a lot of the set up was already in place.

Mosstle realised that when Reed went down to the planet for rebirth, she wouldn't remember who she was or himself. That he found very hard, but as the Elders said, he would be keeping a firm eye on everything from up here.

Jacelet found the idea of loss of memory very hard and wondered how she would know Zude when she met him in the new life. The Elders reassured her that she would know.

"We want you to grow in your own way and achieve your consciousness back again."

"All good for the soul," one Elder laughed.

Flute was furious when she learnt that Zude had stayed in the reptile world. *He should be here with me.*

When she realised he was living a life experience with Danka, she exploded.

"I found that hard as well," Jacelet told her and for once the two of them agreed.

"Well," said Mosstle, "there is hope yet, you two have finally agreed on something."

"But how will Zude come down for a new life?" Reed asked, puzzled.

"The Elders said he was advanced enough to control more than one body at a time," Mosstle said, then added. "Let's just go and enjoy what time we have left, while you still remember."

They left the Great Hall arm in arm.

Jacelet and Flute looked at each other and for once neither had anything to say.

Chapter 9

I was into my eighth summer when the moon lady came for me. I knew she was coming, but not when. She had called last summer when she was travelling through the valley calling at all the homes with young girls. Mother said it was a great honour to be chosen; I was the only girl in our valley to be leaving with the moon lady. I was to take nothing with me, but I knew when you left with the moon lady you never returned. I was sad to leave in some ways, but not so sad. Life was hard here in the valley, especially for the women in the winter when it was so cold. I would not miss the hard work, but I always knew that there was something else for me to do. I felt different from the rest of the family, somehow not quite like I belonged here and something in the back of my mind said that there was more somehow. I had to leave.

Mother, well, she was a strict mother tempered with a little love but now she had Father coming home again and he then he always favoured my brothers. I hardly knew him as he was away so much. So to go with the Moon lady, well, it was an adventure into the unknown. I had been chosen so I was special and was to have a new name, all I knew was that it was to begin with a 'J', and the Moon Lady she was the Lady Reece, respected throughout our country. I would miss my mountains; they were so special to me, reminded me of some other place that was dear to me, but that was all I knew. Here, the tops are always white with snow even in the summer. I hoped there were mountains where I was going.

We travelled three days and I was carried in a litter and never saw where we went.

The heavy curtains were so placed that even daylight had a hard job sneaking through.

I tried to peep out once or twice but was so severally reprimanded that I didn't do it again, but for all that, I was well treated. Frequent stops for food and water, also bodily functions. I had a girl, a few years older than me, to care for all my needs.

Although I spoke to her, she never replied, never spoke at all, and I did so want to talk about the Moon Lady, even the men carrying and guarding our litters never spoke.

It was late in the day when we arrived at our destination; I heard the sound of big gates opening, lots of noise, it all sounded so loud after the silence of my journey.

Suddenly, I missed my mother and the reassurance of a familiar home.

The litter was placed on the ground and the curtains carefully pulled back. The light hurt my eyes and I covered them with my hands. A pair of hands gently removed my hands from my eyes, and a lady with large almond eyes and long black hair that seemed to touch the ground greeted me and hugged me, bid me welcome. She called for two maids to come and take me to my rooms, to bathe, change and feed me, then rest. I thought to myself that I had been in a litter for three days and all I wanted to do was run, shout, sing and see the sky. I always had the feeling that I wanted to be up there like the birds. It was not to be. I was bathed in three lots of water, all smelling nice of herbs then oils massaged into my skin. They shaved my hair off! Saying it was too knotty, and then oils massaged into my scalp, by now I was a little scared, so different to what I was used to. I asked, "Why are you doing this to me and what is it all for?"

It seems I have to have everything from my old life removed before I could start my new life afresh. I would grow new hair for my new way of life.

"Would it still grow back black and straight?" I asked, for some reason it seemed important to me. I was reassured it would be just the same.

I lived in six rooms, placed well inside the compound. I shared with four other girls of my age, we had a large garden where we played, and yes, there were mountains, even more majestic than the ones we had left and we seemed closer to them. I could watch the birds circling and diving, I had such an ache inside me, a need to be with them. Slowly, we drifted into a life where we had lessons in the morning and played in the afternoon; slowly we learned to read and write and then onto other subjects.

A year later, the Moon Lady came to visit, she came to see how we had grown and progressed. She told us that we were now ready to move on to the Silver house where our real training will begin.

So we left our lovely long-haired lady and journeyed on to the Silver house. The Moon Lady said we could spend up to two years here, learning lots of new things.

She is very kind but remote. *Well,* I thought, *at least I am still with three of my friends.* One of my friends, Ky, has gone.

I ask and am told that she didn't pass the test. The Moon Lady's test. *What test?* I thought.

We are to be trained in what and what happened to my friend. They said she hadn't been sent home but had gone to another place more suitable for her needs. Now our days started with scented baths and massages. The maids massaged every part of our bodies under strict instruction from a lady called Suma. She was taller than our last lady and had tight curly hair. She told us that she came from another country by traders and had been sold to this house; she stared as a maid and worked up to being the chief lady. Suma told us that we would have our naming ceremony soon.

Suma explains that we are growing into young ladies and as we grow bodily changes happen, hair grows in different places and our Moon times begin. When that happens we will learn a lot more!!!

We are to be named, we have been here for six months in the silver house and all three of us have our moon times now. We are all dressed in yellow robes and our jet black hair is cut to just below the shoulders. Our names will be special to us, to be used as mantras as we grow into them. I am to be Jute; my two friends are not allowed to tell me their names until they have lived with them for three moons. I hug my name to myself and say it over and over again. Things stir inside me, a mixture of excitement and pain. What does this mean? What is next?

We start to learn more about massages and slowly they become more sensual. I never knew that such pleasure could be had from massage. Suma explains that we must lose ourselves in the pleasure of feeling – the energy it creates is important. We learn about places on our bodies that give joy.

I wonder sometimes where this is all going, what happens next. My old life with Mother is fading, I can hardly see her in my mind. As my childhood fades, so does my old life. Suma is pleased with us; we reach pleasure plateaus and have learned how to please each other. She tells us this is just the beginning of our journey and we still have a long way to go. We have priests who teach us to chant and meditate, but I notice that these are all women. Is this a world of girls and ladies?

Well, we have been in the Silver House for a year and six moons and the Moon Lady comes tomorrow. We are to move to the Golden House, which is even higher up the mountains, almost in the clouds and I love to be near to those high peaks. Of course, we will be leaving Suma who I have grown to love. Suma tells me that I take her love with me, so she will always be with me. She tells me never to be afraid of anything new, that I am a powerhouse of energy and I carry with me the essence of all I have learned. It seems that only Sukel and myself are moving on to the Golden House; our other friend is staying on at the Silver House, to help train new girls. She apparently failed the Moon Lady's tests. I am never aware of any tests.

So Sukel and I walk to the Golden House, amid trumpets blowing, long ones with their bowl part on the ground and lots of flag-waving. I feel shy over so much fuss and why so much fuss? The Moon Lady walks in front of us and the Lady Suma behind. We reach the gates of the Golden House, the Moon Lady walks through, Sukel and I follow, but as I turn to speak to Lady Suma, the gates are shut with her on the other side. I remember what she says about being strong and hold my head up high.

The Moon Lady takes us through into the courtyard to meet our next teacher. A little old lady that has a million years etched upon her face is standing very rigid and erect – she nods to us, she is very regal. The Moon Lady greets her with great respect. To be truthful, I am more than a little scared. We are to call her 'High One', no one is allowed to use her real name, only the Grand Master!

Who is the Grand Master?

There are no servants living in this part of the Golden House and we are to be taught by the 'High One' herself. Our sleeping rooms have doors to the outside courtyards of the Golden House and the servants enter, clean and leave our rooms when we are not there. We see no outsiders; there is only Sukel and myself, plus the little old lady living in this part of the Golden House. We wonder and wait for our next part and wonder what this little old lady can teach.

We are taught to experience pleasure and control in our minds, and the little old lady says when we have mastered that, then we will be taught to bring mind and body together. That energy force will be so strong, so time will pass.

Then one day, the High One started to talk to us about men and their bodies, showing us drawings and explanations. She showed us how their bodies worked, explained how massage worked on them, a hundred and one secrets from this little old lady. She told us about the force and strength created when male and female energies were joined. She taught us the beauty and wonder of the sexual union, with the pleasure of mind and spirit and all its attending power and energy.

I came to love, admire and respect this little old lady and saw far beyond her physical appearance. Her great knowledge of mind and spirit was such that, I, at last, understood why she was called The High One. Although I was still young in years, her teaching expanded me and I finally left childhood behind.

Our year in the Golden House was coming to the end and once more the Moon Lady was due to visit again. She arrived and was in the High One's rooms for a very long time. Then she spoke to Sukel and me, each, at great length. The next day she was to come and take me to the Grand Master; my training was now done and I was ready to take the pathway and walk with the Grand Master. The Moon Lady told me I would learn to love the Grand Master, like they all did, and learn all his ways. I was one of the chosen ones that he would love and the energy would help with the balance of the universe. Sukel also had been chosen, but I would go to him first.

The next morning, the body servants bathed me, anointed me with scented oils, clothed me and prepared me as much as they could for the Grand Master. They treated me with such respect. I didn't expect that. The Moon Lady arrived to take me to the Grand Master. My heart was beating so fast. I hadn't seen a man for over four years.

Trumpets sounded and drums where thumped as the Moon Lady and I set off for the walk to the Inner Temple. I turned to say goodbye to the High One but found she has already returned inside the Golden House. Moon Lady and I set off towards the Inner temple, through three sets of double gates. We entered the Inner Temple and through some splendid rooms to finally come face to face with the Grand Master. I gasped, my stomach turned over and my knees felt weak as I gazed for the first time into the eyes that I seemed to know so well, the eyes of the Grand Master. Some form of recognition passed between us, it was as if I had always known him. Looking at his face, full of love for me, I knew him, and as I felt his energy flood my body, all fear vanished and I was home, truly home. He held his hand out to me in welcome and I grasped it.

"Welcome Jute, I have been waiting for you, I am called Zendal. Come you must meet Florian, it is imperative that you two get on together."

Florian and I looked at each other, again that glimpse of recognition but something else as well. I had a feeling that we wouldn't be quite the best of friends. Sukel was to join us tomorrow and the three of us were to support the Grand Master in all ways, we were to form the first trinity so we all had to get on together. Although there were others who served the Grand Master and had done so for some time, it was the three of us that everyone was waiting for and it was us three that had to form the first foundation.

My new body servants led me off to my rooms and they were to prepare me for my first night with the Grand Master. After seeing him, I knew where I belonged, so I had no fear, just such intense excitement in me that after tonight I would really know what all the years of care, teaching and preparation were about. My only fear was that would I be found not to be adequate. Such responsibility.

Chapter 10

I am not sure if I am shocked or in a state of ecstasy. With all my teachings and preparation, had anything really prepared me for last night.

My skin still felt the imprint of his fingers, it seemed to know his hands so well. My body glowed and I am incapable of any movement or of thought, just lying here, sated and whole. I want no one to come and disturb me, fearing that when they arrive this beautiful place, I am in will disappear, so I wait in limbo. Please no one come and make this all disappear.

The real world reappeared, my body servants arrived to bathe me and dress me. I really do not want them to wash his smell away. Apparently, I am to join Florian for food. The Grand Master today is waiting for Sukel to arrive and she then will be with him till the morrow.

I am suddenly shot through with jealously and I know it is wrong to think like this but I hope he doesn't find her enchanting or enjoyable. How bad am I? We have to work together, the three of us, with the Grand Master. So I must put all bad thoughts from my head and Sukel is such a lovely person, very gentle but strong. I am sure she would not have such thoughts.

Now for Florian, I know she has such thoughts, I knew the moment both of us saw each other. I knew her because we are alike.

When I arrived in the hall of leisure, the Moon Lady was there, as well as Florian. The two were in a deep discussion and it took a moment or two before they noticed me. Holding her hands out to me, the Moon Lady pulled me into an embrace; her beautiful red hair tumbled out over my shoulders and we laughed together as she folded it back into place. I greeted Florian warmly but saw a look in her eyes and knew at that moment she had been suffering jealously over me. For a moment that pleased me. How alike we were. The Moon lady explained that now her search for us was over, that she now had no need to search the valleys each year and had enough backups if it all went wrong. I was rather taken aback at this piece of information. I don't want anyone taking my place if anything goes wrong.

"What could go wrong?"

The Moon Lady laughed at my expression saying, "It is up to you three to see that nothing goes wrong and remember you have to work together and now I am here to help you balance yourselves, and I will be known as the Lady Reece."

Suddenly, the clamour of horns and cymbals boomed through the Hall and I knew that Sukel had arrived. My stomach clenched and I looked at Florian and was pretty sure hers had done the same. I half grinned at her, at least we agree over something. I laughed and she grinned back.

Whereupon Florian would love to boast what she and Zute did in bed, so I used to try and better what she said. Suekel never ever said what went on between them, keeping it all very quiet and that used to annoy both of us.

Lady Reece started taking us through why we should control our emotions. She explained to us that through sexual union with our Zute our energy was being expanded all of the time; being very valuable energy for balance in the universe, it so important to keep the balance with the positive in ascendancy, so greater control over our emotions was required. We listened but I do not think that we related this to our behaviour, perhaps we did not want to really listen.

Thinking about it all, I do not think that neither Florian nor I really wanted to control our jealously or anger, both wanting Zute for ourselves and was not really relating to all our training and knowledge of what we did to help balance the universe, to save it from destruction. This thought rang a bell in my head. I had vague memories of another life, another time when we were fleeing danger and climbing some sort of web, but here it all faded and I felt it had all ended badly, all because of Florian and myself. I couldn't pinpoint the exact details. In one of our more friendly moments, I tried to discuss this with Florian, but she either didn't know or didn't share my memories. So while we also laughed together in these moments, both of us were still suffering from jealously so I should have not been surprised with what came next.

Several years had passed, and although the work of sexual energy went well and was used well in the balancing aspects. Florian and I still stopped any great progression with our possessiveness and jealously that flowed between us. Apparently, this was becoming a concern to the Elders.

I didn't know who these elders were or why they had the greater say over the work we were all doing. I know Zute sat in a meditative state and left his body to meet these Elders in conference. I know he always stood up for Florian and me, saying we would be better soon. I knew myself inside that I should be in better control, but then I observed Florian talking and coercing people to believe the worse of me. She was so clever that others believe the lies she said about me and of course, drip-feeding of lies and tales slowly started to take hold. I would notice how the others would watch me. Even Lady Reece seemed to be watching me. This hurt as I loved and admired the Lady Reece.

Zute's plan was to take both Florian and I together in sexual ritual so that both of us would know and observe what went on with each other and we then were forced into the position of working together. Zute was always saying that the love he had for each of us was for ourselves alone and neither love detracted anything from the other. So while the three of us worked together like this, the lies that Florian had been telling faded away.

Till there came a time when I was required to be on my own with Zute as it was my particular energy that was required for a universal job. So Zute and I were together for some time. At the end of these days, I was so exhausted that the Lady Reece came and collected me with my body servants to carry me back to my rooms.

Although she was so kind to me, I knew something was up and it wasn't until later when Sukel visited me to warn me of what Florian had been up to. She had spread tales of me, of how when Zute was with Sukel and herself I was off seeking sexual satisfaction with any of the body servants. Florian had proof, she had said of how I was sullying my energy and putting Zute and everyone in negative danger. The Elders had heard of this and I was to be investigated.

I was furious and scared. I knew what punishments were handed out to lesser faults. Sukel said to me to be careful and not to add to the discord.

She had been on her way to be with Zute when he had been summoned to go before the Elders.

Although exhausted, I set off to find the Lady Reece at her rooms; her body servant said she had been summoned to go before the Elders. Now I was really quite scared and mad with the injustice, it was all getting out of hand. That was it. I turned and made my way to Florian's rooms.

Her body servants blocked the entrance to her rooms. This made me so mad that energy grown out of fear and hate took me over; pushing my way past the servants, I found and faced Florian. I accused her of her deceit and she laughed at me saying, "I got you this time."

I grabbed her, shook her and she laughed louder. I grabbed a metal bowl off the table and hit and hit and hit her and the laughter stopped.

The day dawned bright, Sukel was doing my hair. Quietly and sadly, she plaited and drew it over my right shoulder. When done, with tears escaping her eyes she hugged me and kissed me.

I could say nothing, my tongue had been removed. Silently, my body servants lead me out into the arena. I was tied to a post with my hands behind my back. I looked around at the people watching, searching for Zute, for one last glance of him. He was not there.

The sun shone and I looked up at my favourite mountains. A shadow in front of me brought me back to the arena. There was Zute, approaching me with a ceremonial knife; he bought it up to my throat.

Chapter 11

The hall was abuzz with discussion and one elder was talking to another and quickly moving on to talk to another; it was a cacophony of sound and electric energy. Zude stood in his true form just amazed at all the trouble his two Queens had caused. Mosstle resting his hand on Zude's shoulder stated, "Between us all, we will make it alright, we will get those Queens of yours on the right track."

Reed stood up between the two friends and slipped her arms into theirs.

"It's serious, I know. I think the elders thought one lifetime might change it all, I think we need a few!"

The three of them sat in the allotted place and waited for the process to begin.

Flute and Jacelet arrived both looking assuredly ashamed. Standing in their true form with all memory restored, both really didn't know where to look or what to say.

Mosstle stood and waited for acknowledgement from the Wise One.

"I stand in defence of Flute and Jacelet. This we must remember is an experiment, never done before. Placing any one in a world alien to us all here and taking away their memories of their true self and other lives would devastate anyone here. We know it is essential that control is learned.

"The balance of that universe is of utmost importance. We cannot afford to lose another universe. To block off all knowledge is a massive action. So I vote that at least another five lifetimes are required and also we help by restoring a little memory each life to assist in their battle with the energies."

As Mosstle spoke, many other entities took their place by Mosstle, many of them from the reptilian world led by Danka. Many who knew and loved Zude also showed their support.

The Wise One acknowledged this and turned to mentally confer with the Elders. Complete silence filled the hall, even the reptilians were hushed.

In the silence, the Wise One spoke. He acknowledged the wisdom of Mosstle and was taking this to heart. Since some advancement in opening up the consciousness had happened with all concerned in the life just lived, and so, because of these facts, the experiment would continue and the Elders will assist more. For each advancement made, they would open up more memory for Flute and Jacelet and all others that are there in each particular life experience. So on to the next life.

This battle had been going on for some time. Even Zaire was feeling the strain. He was wounded by a sword wound on his left thigh, although this was only slight, the constant trickle of blood was annoying as much as weakening. Faisel and Sasiel were fighting strongly at his side, sisters close enough in age to look like twins. His two feisty wives. Their coffee coloured skin was smeared with blood, not their own he was glad to note. It was time for him and his close group to drop back and let his second in command take charge.

As he signalled to his group to retreat and before they could move out of the way, the enemy made a sudden great leap forward. Lead by two people, leaping and screaming as they surged forward, the female of the two let an arrow fly hitting Zaire in the arm. For a moment, their eyes met and something passed between them. Then they were parted in the scream of battle.

Zaire was having the arrow removed from his left arm, the memory of the woman's dark eyes stayed with him.

There she is, he thought. *How is this going to come about.* Pondering on these thoughts, he fell into an exhausted deep asleep.

Later that night, Faisel and Sasiel, having had their wounds dressed, crawled into the bed with Zaire. Briefly, he awoke, then as they settled down either side of him, Zaire fell back into slumber mumbling, "How is this going to happen," as a pair of dark eyes filled his mind.

It was midmorning before the trio stirred, each one waking to a moan and a groan. Zaire leapt up suddenly shouting, "How is the battle going?"

One of his men appeared in the tent opening.

"Hush, my lord, the battle is long over and victory is ours. We have some interesting captives to decide what to do with. Rest, my lord."

He clapped his hands and a young girl appeared carrying three goblets.

"Drink and rest, my lord."

Zaire looked down at his thigh as a trickle of blood ran down his leg.

"Rest, my lord."

"That is good," said Zaire as he drunk the contents down in one gulp and fell back onto the covers with a sigh, instantly asleep again and the girls just as quick, followed suit.

Meanwhile, a pair of dark eyes and tight curly hair was bent over the head of a young man. Rocking him backwards and forwards chanting a mournful sound.

"Another live one here."

Grabbing the tight curly hair roughly, pulling her away from the still young man, saying, "Another one, for the slave master."

He walked on dragging her and pulling out handfuls of hair as she screamed, kicked; trying hard to reach back for her young love.

"Noooooooooooooo."

Silence came as a cruel slap sliced across her face and her limp body was pulled away, leaving a trail of blood.

After the battle, there was a feeling of inertia, warriors talking about cut and thrust and how lucky they were to escape injury, while others nursed their injuries saying how lucky they were to be alive, then when rested, not knowing what really to do with themselves.

It was into this situation that Zaire decided it was time to move camp.

Whether to the highlands and the mountains or lowlands with grasslands and waterways, which was on the way to the rich lands before the desert. Their normal winter stop.

Which was it to be? They usually moved when climate dictated which way to go, so this was a different decision as they would normally stay on the Steppes longer.

They would take the prisoners with them, making use of them on the move, carrying the heavy stuff. This gave the women of the tribe an unusual break and Zaire knew many were still suffering with their wounds.

Work began to gather in the horses, goats and camels. Many of these were scattered because of the battle and took some time to locate.

A buzz filled the camp as with renewed interest everyone fell into and played their part in packing everything.

Zaire sat in a ring around the fire discussing with his second in command, Xavier. As they both rubbed their hands to warm them and Zaire looked at the rest of his leaders.

"I was thinking of the mountains but looking at how everyone here looks so weary, I think we will go south for a while. Have some warmth and healing time, before heading back to the mountains."

Xavier nodded his head in agreement and all the other leaders acquiesced.

Xavier stood and said, "It is a good time to check the slaves, have our pick before the rest of the tribe get theirs." Zaire nodded.

Zaire stood in front of the girl. A pair of dark eyes glared at him with hate and anger. He looked at her matted hair and her body stained with blood and other battle debris. Despite her animosity, Zaire was aware she was puzzled by the energy that had passed between them. Zaire's thoughts were tossing between two options, he could take her and he knew all hell would let loose or walk on by and keep his reasonable balanced life with his two wives.

He sighed, he knew what was right.

A pair of wilful dark eyes was left standing amidst the packed luggage of Zaire's goods and servers. A rough rope around her neck held by a man who several years ago was also a battle trophy.

"Do as you are told girl and I will treat you right. You belong to Zaire now and until I know what he wants of you, you will obey me."

She spat at him.

"Ah, you do understand me." He laughed.

A week of travel brought them to a vast green vista with a river running through and warmth in the air, it was decided that this would be their resting and recovery place for as long as necessary, or until the warmth turned to heat and they retreated back to the mountains. So all set out to make this place home. Everyone was glad to have somewhere to settle and recuperate.

A pair of dark eyes stood sullenly, watching everyone happily working to raise the tents and organise areas of cooking, eating, and the animals glad to rest and have some freedom. She watched wondering what was going to happen to her and still grieving for her loss of her young man. Her neck was sore from the rope, but her pride would never say so. She was dirty and her hair crawled. Her sores had begun to fester, but she had not been ill-treated, just neglected and ignored.

Two serving women came for her and took her down to the river. When the remains of her clothes were stripped away, the three of them entered the river.

The water was cold but it felt so good on her body. The women scrubbed her till she was almost raw. They cut off all her hair and she watched as it floated away in the current; at last, she began to feel clean. Her wounds dressed, her feet attended to, clean clothes on her body. What next?

New Life, New name. She now belonged to Zaire, forget her old life!

Never that would be denying her young man; he was the love of her life and Zaire killed him. Never the dark eyes flashed.

Jacquill, the owner of the dark eyes, was standing in front of Zaire. He was speaking, Jacquill wasn't listening; she was wrapped up in her thoughts of revenge – how dare he kill her young man. Battle or no battle, he still took him away from her.

Zaire looked at the dark eyes. *She is not hearing me*, he thought.

He looked at the black curly hair starting to grow back, at the body that was healing well. He felt a rush of great love for her and at the same time, a sadness that she did not recognise him.

Jacquill lifted her eyes, suddenly aware that he had stopped talking and was watching her. He was looking at her in a way that seemed vaguely familiar and she felt a shot of energy flood her body, which took her by such surprise, that she staggered for a moment where she stood. Their eyes met and locked for a moment. Jacquill, just as suddenly, shook her head and thought, *How dare he!*

Late that night, Zaire took and bedded his two wives Faisel first then Sasiel and then Faisel, again. As long as he always took Faisel first and then again last, peace reigned with his two wives. The two sisters got on well and it never bothered Sasiel that Faisel always needed to be more important and to be always loved first and again after Zaire had made love with her.

Zaire again pondered on bringing into this threesome another wife to be.

He knew Sasiel would accept, but Faisel, well, he must be mad to upset their comfortable world, but needs must, he sighed again.

Well one day Faisel and Jacquill will have to get on together, *So bring it on* he thought, *but I will miss the comfort of the current arrangement.* He decided that for the moment he will say nothing.

Jacquill was waiting in Zaire's chamber; she had been washed, perfumed and dressed by a body servant and left here in Zaire's place, with a guard at the entrance. *Is that to keep me in or stop others coming in,* she pondered. Over the past weeks, she had observed Zaire's wives and was well aware of Faisel's possessiveness and of Sasiel's acceptance.

So was she well aware what her presence in all their lives will do. Well, she didn't care less, as she did not love Zaire, only her young man who was so very dead, so whatever happened didn't matter as far as she was concerned. She would fight Zaire every inch of the way.

"He did what," screamed Faisel. "He took who, when did he do this. I'll kill her. Wait till I get my hands on her."

"If you throw any more platters, we will have none left to eat off," remarked Sasiel.

"Why aren't you mad?" Yelled Faisel.

"No need, you yell enough for both of us, besides it is Zaire's right to take another."

"Not without asking me first," spat Faisel.

"Would you have agreed?"

"No, I would not."

Saisel threw her arms up in the air, sighed and left Faisel in the midst of the mess she had made.

Zaire was well aware of the ruckus that was going on and kept himself busy and out of the girls' way. He had Jacquill hidden and guarded until he thought it safe to bring them all together. He had just spent another night with Jacquill and was concerned that she still fought him. He knew that she had recognised him when they first met but was sad she was blocking this off and resisting him as much as she could. Unconsciously, he rubbed the scratch marks covering his arms.

Well, Zaire thought with grim humour he was getting it from both sides.

What had he unleashed? With that thought, he sent a message to Sasiel to come to his tent. *I need a bit of comfort and peace,* he thought to himself before he made his next move. He was going to create mayhem.

Jacquill and Faisel stood opposite each other each glaring daggers at the other.

"What are you doing here?" Yelled Faisel.

Equally forceful, Jacquill shouted, "None of your business."

"Well, I am here. So just go. Did you hear me? Just Go! Go before I do…"

"Do what, Faisel?" Zaire stood with arms akimbo. "Do what?"

In two strides and he grabbed Faisel's wrists, "Do what?"

He pulled her down she tumbled down onto a pile of cushions.

Grabbing Jacquill's wrists turned to throw her down, but she was ready and jumped straight up again.

"Down," said Zaire. "Get down now."

Faisel watched with a weird fascination as Zaire forced Jacquill down and spread himself over her.

"We will take all night; if it takes force or you can both enjoy what is to happen. It will happen, it has to happen and you two will learn. Together you learn."

Zaire sat up between them and looked at each one.

"We start with you each of you undressing each other, with care. Now."

Zaire watched the pair with a wry grin as they gingerly disrobed each other. Each looking at the other's body trying not to like what they saw.

"Now undress me, both of you, for I am so ready, but we will take this slow."

The three lay down caressing each other, the girls haltingly, with each other at first, but as Zaire stimulated them both, it became more intense.

At last, thought Zaire, as the three energies mixed, *maybe this might work.*

He tossed Faisel over on all fours and entered her and while Jacquill stood over Faisel with her hands on her shoulders and her sex facing Zaire's mouth. *At last*, he thought as his tongue sought her bud, and with increasing rhythms brought both girls to their first climax and then with each girl swapping places, slowly reached their second of many to come.

The threesome slept late into the morning. All exhausted but sated. Zaire was the first to stir and gently pulled himself out of the tangle of limbs. He took a moment to look at the entwined pair and with a sigh hoped this was the beginning of some coming together, but he knew his girls well. It might take a lot more yet. He slipped out of the tent and went in search of Sasiel.

Soon it would be time to move off towards the mountains. Wounds were healing and people were getting over the tensions of the battle. Captives sorted.

They had not kept many of them, selling them off to other traders as they passed by the camp. Zaire recognised that he needed with him people loyal to him and it takes time to win captives over and with the trek to the mountains looming, he needed everyone's concentration on the task ahead.

It was hard enough keeping tabs on Jacquill. There was something in her demeanour that told him that there was still trouble ahead. He loved the bones of hers, but knew that though she recognised him, she would not admit it to herself. Although, when in a sexual situation, their energies all flowed well together, at other times, there was an uneasy peace between Jacquill and Faisel. Sasiel, bless her, spent her time constantly balancing the other two. Ah well, time will tell.

With relief, Zaire watched the slow appearance of the mountains, it had been quite a journey.

What with the conflict between Jacquill and Faisel, the constant bickering, each trying to put the other down, that had wearied him. Zaire sighed, the mountains always calmed his spirit, reminded him of some home and life long ago. He was glad the journey's end was in sight. Perhaps leaving the plain's heat will cool his ladies down. He kicked his horse with his heels and galloped off to the front of the caravan. First up into the cooler air, he felt lighter and freer. As he rode, he pondered upon the decisions that he had made while on the trail. He smiled wirily to himself, he was about to cause more trouble, but it was the only way he could think of that would make Jacquill see.

He rode well past where the campsite was to be, up into the cool of the mountain air, into the mist. He shivered but the cool was balm to his spirit.

He dropped off his grey horse. She was new to him and he still hadn't found a suitable name. Zaire missed his old stallion that had died almost at the start of the long journey, maybe this horse was too light for him. He laughed to himself, light in colour and light in size. Perhaps a good horse for Jacquill to ride.

Sometime later, Zaire arrived back at the camp to find it all up and running. It struck him how long he had been out on his own. Well, time to put his decisions into being.

When it came to evening, Zaire only sent for the two sisters to be his bed partners, leaving Jacquill to puzzle over why she hadn't been called. This went on all week, and at mealtimes, Zaire made a great fuss over Faisel and Sasiel, at the same time, ignoring the presence of Jacquill. At first, Jacquill was just miffed and thought, *good, I won't have to put with his advances anymore,* but as the week went on, her body started to ache from the absence of Zaire's touch. She began to miss his energy, his lovemaking, the feeling of completeness, the sated feeling in the morning. It dawned on her that she missed him, that was a big shock to her system, but she certainly was not going to let him know how she felt.

Meanwhile, Faisel was delighted. *At last,* she thought *he has given her up and he is all mine again. Won't be long before he gives her to one of his captains or better still sells her. But whom to, when they are isolated in their mountain camp.*

Zaire was watching Jacquill's every reaction and realised that her pride would not let her admit to missing him. Zaire was surprised that he missed her greatly, but needs must. *Another week*, he thought.

It was another three weeks before Jacquill lost her cool disdain and at one meal time flew into a frustrated rage at Zaire as he made such a fuss of Faisel.

She pounded Zaire with her fists and to Faisel's amazement, Zaire just grabbed her, threw her over his shoulder and strode out of the tent with a yelling protesting Jacquill.

Within five minutes of Zaire taking Jacquill with some fierceness, Jacquill was returning her ardour with equal force. In the midst of passion, Zaire acknowledged to himself his surprise of her passion and the pleasure of her no longer fighting him. *Job done,* he thought and gave himself fully to Jacquill.

Faisel was fuming that neither of the pair turned up for the last meal of the day and as night slowly passed, it was clear that Zaire had no need for Faisel that night. Sasiel just laughed and said everything would be back to being the three of them again. Faisel just privately vowed she would get Jacquill, somehow. She would bide her time but just wait.

Summer passed quickly and the three girls got on well and did their work of blending energies with Zaire's well. It seemed to be all alright but Zaire was a little uneasy of the vibes he was picking up from Faisel. Every now and then on the surface she seemed fine, their conjoined lovemaking was good and she showed no hesitancy when it was all of them combined.

The heat of the plains was abating and the mountain camp was cooling.

It was time to pack up and move the long journey to the spot where the green plains turned into the wildness of the edge of the Steppes.

The journey back to the green plains passed quickly and quite uneventfully.

For that point alone, Zaire was thankful. He rode with his leaders in the day. The journey was full of ribald jokes and laughter and the nights were full of love and laughter. Zaire could barely believe it all, perhaps at last his girls had learnt!

It seemed that in no time at all they had arrived at the plains and the river that showed its stony bottom. They crossed and set up the camp on the other side. This was their normal winter camp, although the was ground arid and river low, with winter coming it would soon be all green and water plenty.

They struck their camp between a ridge, which protected the camp from the strong winds that blew up from the Steppes, and enough distance from the river that would swell.

It always had been a safe choice.

With the camp safely erected, it was time to think of stocking the larder. The large pit that they used for storage had been checked and cleaned up and was all ready for use.

The organised hunt was huge, everyone played a part, from looking for edible grasses and berries to any animals they could shoot to those who would prepare all meats and food when the others returned.

Sasiel was going with foragers, Faisel and Jacquill joined the search for meat. Zaire had a new stronger mount and to Jacquill's delight, the grey was now hers, and with her quiver on her back and knife in her sash, she was eager to start. Excitement was in the air, everyone eager to be off. The riders went off in separate directions in groups of four or five to cover as much ground as they could.

No one seemed to know what happened, no one saw, but Jacquill took the arrow in her breast and her grey horse broke its leg in a fall over a steep ridge. The horse was destroyed on the spot but was to be taken back for food, for nothing could be wasted. Xavier had heard the horse scream and came across Jacquill injured half under her horse. She was alone no one else in sight. He took her onto his horse, left orders for his men to deal with the horse and searched around for signs of who had been there.

He rode fast but carefully, his aim to find Zaire. The news had travelled fast and before he reached the camp saw Zaire riding from another direction, with Faisel and Sasiel in hot pursuit. Zaire leapt from his horse as it skidded to a halt, stumbling in his haste, he reached for Jacquill.

Xavier gently lowed her into Zaire's arms.

The medicine man shook his head, Zaire moaned deep in his soul.

"The arrow came clean out but caught on something vital on its way in and I am afraid it is only a matter of hours.

Although it is only seeping, I cannot stop the flow." The medicine man left after giving Jacquill something for the pain.

"She will feel nothing," he had said and left Zaire and his women to attend to Jacquill.

"Leave her," he snapped at the others and he gathered Jacquill into his arms, holding her gently but closer to himself, murmuring softly into her ears, how much he loved her and not to leave him. Then shouting at the gods for allowing this to happen.

All night Zaire walked, sat and rocked with Jacquill in his arms, bemoaning at the gods, holding her close in an act of deep love. As dawn broke, she took her last breath. Zaire yelled out in despair, and still, he walked and held onto her although, she was long gone. It was many hours later that Xavier, at last, managed to get Zaire to relinquish Jacquill into the arms of those who will care for her last bodily needs.

All this was watched by a distraught Sasiel. Sobbing as she watched Zaire, feeling his pain every inch of the way, knowing there was nothing she could do to ease his pain. A sobbing Faisel watched too, angry though at the way Zaire was caring for Jacquill, but with the tears shed, there was a small guarded smile.

Chapter 12

Hustle bustle, constant movement, uproar and heated discussion. Never had the Elders' Chamber seen so much discord. Entities were taking sides.

Zude turned to Mosstle, "I cannot believe my ladies have again caused so much trouble, it's unknown here to have so much discord."

Mosstle looked around, "Where are they? I haven't seen them since you all returned."

At that point, finally, the wise one held his hand up. Everyone at once held a respectable silence.

"The last life has been again not quite what we hoped and planned. Again, some progress has been made, but certainly not as much as we had anticipated. What is tragic is that Flute orchestrated Jacelet's death when it seemed to be going well."

Mosstle felt Zude blanch.

"You didn't know," Mosstle said. Zude looked at him with such deep sadness in his eyes.

"No, I didn't know."

"So what the council has decided is there will be a life with no Jacelet. A luxury life which will become a difficult life with a lot of restrictions and we will see how Flute handles it all."

With that said and done the Wise One slowly faded and was gone, leaving the chamber in an uproar.

Zude was instantly summoned to a pre-life gathering with all that were going to partake. Turing to Mosstle and holding his friends arm, Zude said, "Can you see that Jacelet is aware that I would have loved to say farewell to her, but looks like I will not get a chance."

"Of course, my friend, it will be done."

Reed appeared and hugged both Mosstle and Zude, saying to Zude, "I have been summoned; it seems I am to be with you somehow in this next life."

Zude took Reed's hand and kissed her fingers and turning to Mosstle said, "I will take good care of your lady," and shook Mosstle's hand who jokingly replied, "You better."

"I will certainly try, but from what I gather, it seems I am to have restricted memory this next life."

She really was the most beautiful girl he had ever seen. It hit him hard in the solar plexus. He, a battle-hardened soldier, who took women when and where he wanted, was smitten and in love instantly. Zafar had just been posted to the palace and was to be in the battalion that guarded the palace. He watched her walk down the corridor, her long black hair swinging and swaying like a black silk curtain. Who was she? She would never notice me, thought Zafar.

Oh, but she noticed the tall sunburnt man with broad shoulders. He stood so erect, so sure of himself. Oh yes, she had noticed him all right and then pretended she hadn't. Princess Falon walked down the long corridor letting her hair swing, knowing this man was watching her every move.

Zafar went to report to his new commander. When Zafar first knew he was to be part of the palace guard, he had been sorely disappointed. He really liked the cut and thrust of battle and the wide-open spaces. He thought he could not possibly enjoy the confines of a royal posting.

That, of course, was before he saw her! Who was she? Zafar only half-listened to his new commander as he outlined Zafar's duties.

Commander Marcus was saying that at first Zafar might find it all rather tame, but every soldier in the Royal army had to do at least a year of palace duties and he expected the year would soon pass, then Zafar could choose whichever regiment he wanted.

Zafar's first weeks flew by, he was very busy learning his way around the palace, the different rota duties and the royals he was to protect. He never saw his beautiful girl who had captured his heart at all. He began to wonder if he had imagined her. Where was she, was she one of the handmaidens that served the royal ladies? Was she only visiting? If so, how would he locate her? Was he ever going to see her again? For some reason, he was inexplicably drawn to her. Some faint memory stirred in his mind, Zafar shook his head as the memory slipped away and escaped him.

Princess Falon was, in fact, on her annual visit to her mother's family with her two elder sisters, staying with their Grand Mere for a whole month. Princes Falon could not get Zafar out of her mind. He just lodged there, like it was his natural place. Who was he? Would he still be at the palace when she returned? Princess Falon's mind was far away and when Grand Mere talked, she did not hear. Grand Mere was wise, she wondered if it was one of the young men that had been presented at the palace recently that had perhaps caught her eye.

Four Persian princes had been bought forth for the three sisters to choose whom they would like and with that, grand hopes of a marriage alliance with Persia and a peace treaty between the two countries.

The month at Grand Mere's palace seemed to drag on for Princess Falon.

Normally, she loved the visits, but she was so besotted by Zafar and worried constantly about finding him again that she really couldn't wait for it all to end.

Zafar had just come off duty and was returning to his quarters when the trumpets sounded. The massive gates groaned and swung open. First to enter was the walking guards, following them came several litters. When they reached the grand staircase that swept up to the entrance, they stopped and out stepped several young women. In the middle of these, was Zafar's dream girl. He stood transfixed as she passed by him, elegantly climbing the grand staircase. Zafar's heart was beating so loudly that he was sure it was heard by everyone present. Zafar grabbed one of the servants, pointing urgently as he said, "Who is that girl? Whose handmaiden is she?"

The palace servant pushed Zafar's arm down with rough force saying, "Don't look, it is forbidden to stare. That's the Princess Falon, the youngest daughter of the royal household."

Zafar was shocked, rooted to the ground, she was of royal blood. Deflated he turned and with bent shoulders headed to his quarters.

Princess Falon saw this beautiful young man on the stairs, she watched him turn, dejectedly and walk away. She turned to her handmaiden and said, "Who is that? Find out for me."

Later that evening, as she was being bathed and perfumed, her handmaiden came with her clean linen and said to Princess Falon, "That young man you asked about is just a palace guard, your highness, no one of importance."

Princess Falon replied, "Non-royal blood."

The handmaiden replied, "No one of any importance."

The weeks passed painfully, both Zafar and the princess would catch glimpses of each other around the palace. Princess Falon would take her walks in the areas that she knew she would find Zafar on duty. Carefully, she lovingly would gaze at him, craving for his touch. Imagining his fingers running down her spine. Longing for his touch, she thought she was careful, but someone was always watching!

Zafar, when he saw the Princess walking towards him, kept his eyes downcast, but his eyes had a life of their own. They would watch her every move, drinking her in into the very fibre of his soul. Zafar was sure no one noticed and that he was in full control of the situation.

Zafar went to see his commander asking about a transfer, he had to leave before it drove him all mad. He was told that he had to do his year's duty and that was that. The Commander then said, "In fact, I was about to send for you as you are to be made part of Princess Falon's personal bodyguard. You will take up your new duties tomorrow. Now, dismiss."

Zafar was shattered, how was he going to be able to guard the Princess without giving himself away. How was he going to get away with not showing any feeling? Troubled, he left.

Falon was delighted; he was to be her own personal bodyguard – amazing.

She was so excited that she rushed to find Rachmid, her lifelong body servant. Of course, she was horrified by the Princess' outburst.

"You must guard your looks and never show any emotion," Rachmid firmly said. "It's forbidden. You know what they would do to you if anyone found out."

Falon laughed at Rachmid warnings.

"We are quite safe here in my quarters."

All her life she had been safe and cosseted, after all, she was of royal blood, no one in her short life had ever said 'No'.

Each day Falon would include Zafar in her activities, pulling him into light-hearted banter. Sometimes she would touch his arm when he passed close to her, even brushed his hand fleetingly. The other courtiers and servants gathered a barrier around them. They thought they were safe, but someone was watching and just waiting.

Rachmid was really very frightened for her mistress.

"You know what the priests would do to you both if they find out?" cried Rachmid.

The Princess thought she was safe and cocooned in her protected environment.

The King sent for his three daughters, he told them that they were all to be married to the Princes of Persia, as there were four of them, they could have their own choice. It was to be a good alliance. The King always mindful of his three daughters, asked if any of them had a preference out of the four Princes. Falon's elder sisters delighted that they had been allowed a choice, each stated who they would like. Princess Falon shouted that she didn't like any of them and didn't want to get married anyway. The King was really angry over this saying that she had no choice but to marry one of the princes, the agreement had been signed and he would choose who would be her husband. They were all to leave in six months' time for Persia for the grand weddings and an even grander alliance.

So she had better get used to the idea. Falon was devastated, she had no choice but to obey her father.

That night Falon told Zafar. He knew that there was nothing they could do; they couldn't run away, they couldn't declare their love for that meant torture and death for both. As the night wore on, the comfort Zafar gave to Falon slowly turned into gentle kisses and fluttery caresses, and suddenly the dam broke and all reason was gone. Zafar took Falon, in their wild passion, love and lust rolled into one. Lost in one another, their passion knew no boundaries and finally sated, they fell into a deep contented sleep.

They gave no thought to those who watched and knew.

Every night they made love, not caring anymore about the consequences of their actions. They joined joyously together, passion and lust closely bonded, deep and strong in each other's soul. Rachmid, with the help of some other handmaidens, kept the secret and protected where they could.

Meanwhile, Falon, knowing she had to leave for Persia, wanted, needed and craved every stolen moment she and Zafar could take. He was her very soul, she could no more stop herself than to stop two halves of a magnet. Zafar knew that wherever Falon was, that was where he wanted to be, there was no other place.

Rachmid watched and carefully observed everyone who came into contact with the Princess. She was so fearful for her mistress; she had been with her since babyhood and had been trained as her body servant for life.

It was one of these times of watchfulness that she noticed that one of the Princess's bodyguards (a friend of Zafar's) was displaying jealously and anger, it infused his face for an unguarded moment. In a flash, the look was gone. Rachmid noticed that whenever Zafar and Falon got together, Xamus was never far away! Quietly observing, trying to control the violent emotion that periodically flitted across his face.

Rachmid was so frightened by these events that she begged the Princess and Zafar to stop, to be apart, while there was still time.

Xamus could stand it no longer; his hatred of Zafar outweighed his love of Falon. Jealously overtook his reason. He took his knowledge to the King.

The King was shattered, he loved his youngest daughter, but laws were laws and the priests would not bend. He wanted proof, lots of proof, so one by one the Princess's courtiers and handmaidens were taken for questioning. Rachmid, who had been watching Xamus, watched with horror as secretly, one by one, they were taken away for questioning. She knew the end had come for the lovers. For to those who broke the vows, the priests were harsh. First, their sex was roughly, brutally cut away, sometimes they made the lovers do the deed to each other. Then they were killed very slowly with the death of the thousand cuts.

Rachmid learnt that the guards were coming for her mistress and Zafar that evening where they would be found together. Rachmid had to be very careful for the guards were looking for her as well and she had things she must arrange. Quickly, Rachmid found and consulted with the wise old woman.

When the priests and guards arrived that evening, marching forcefully into the Princess' quarters, they arrested the last few remaining handmaidens and forced, their way into the bed chamber where they found Falon and Zafar in each other's arms, not in passion, but in death.

Poisoned by the faithful Rachmid, who also had taken the same poison and lay across the end of the bed so to be near, in death, to her beloved Princess and her true life's love.

Chapter 13

"Well," said Mosstle, "that was quite a difficult life experience you had with Flute. I hope she now fully understands the connection between you two, and how that connection cannot be broken, whatever else happens."
He shook Zude's hand, then they embraced fiercely.

"I must say that it is nice to be back." Reed said happily. "Am I glad that that life is over, quite gruelling at times, especially as we all had no memory of here, I am so glad to be back with you."

Mosstle turned and engulfed Reed with his long arms.

"I am so glad to have you back as well." He mumbled quietly while nuzzling her neck.

"How is Jacelet, have you seen much of her? Must find her before the judgement meeting."

Zude strode off before Mosstle could answer.

Laughing, he looked at Reed, "He is in a bit of hurry and I am in a bit of hurry to have you all to myself."

Reed added, "Flute has been taken for a deep sleep and life review, so we all have some time to ourselves before we are summoned for the reckoning."

Elsewhere, Zude and Jacelet were very involved in some catching up of their own.

Another crowded hall, entities overflowing into the aisles, finding any space to observe what would happen next was difficult.

"This has caused such great interest. Never before has a group such as ours has had to go through so many tests and strange earth lives."

Having said that; Mosstle settled himself down beside Reed and took her hand.

She looked at him and said, "This is all so important, for it all helps for what we have to do afterwards."

Mosstle nodded and watched as Zude arrived with Jacelet and Flute.

Overhearing what was said, laughingly he said, "We shouldn't have joined," and all of them fell around laughing.

"What choice did we have," spluttered Mosstle.

A silence fell over all and the expected Wise One materialised on the round stone.

As one, all stood in deep respect.

"The Elders and I have followed the events of the last life with diligence and have come to the decision that all that had happened was for the good of Flute realising that in a physical body, with mental and spiritual restrictions, just how strong the connection was between her and Zude. In her deep sleep it was found that her subconscious had realised the strength of that connection between her and Zude, and a dawning of it being unbreakable was born. We therefore agree, confidently, that we can go ahead with the next life as was planned with Jacelet, Flute and Sukel harmoniously backing Zude. There will be no rest break and the participants will start the new life immediately."

A small groan arose for Mosstle and Zude.

"Knowing your ladies, Zude, I expect it will be a life with a short expectation, so I have spoken, it will be immediate," the Wise One forcefully said.

Mosstle and Zude stood and bowed in acquiescence.

Zude, Jacelet, Flute and Sukel stood in the ring at the Hall of Endeavor, the place of all arrivals and departures. Looking at his three ladies, hoping in his heart all will be well, he said, "Well, here we go again, not sure how much memory we will all have, so here's to us all doing well." And they all kissed each other.

My Lord and Master is called Zannard and I adore him, will love him forever. My name is Jasander and I am one with Zannard. My worst problem is that I am second lady and Zannard has three of us. Under our laws, Zannard could have up to ten ladies, but Zannard says three, like us, are more than enough for him.

Floris is number one. She is strong limbed and darker-skinned than I, her hair curls neatly around her head, not like mine, which is long and straight. Floris always fights at Zannard's right side, and I, Jasander, take my place on Zannard's left, next to his heart.

(I try to convince myself, that this makes me more dear to him.) Suelyn always follows on behind Zannard, as she always protects him from behind. No one is allowed to harm Zannard. We make a strong fighting unit.

I often use short swords, held like daggers, one in each hand, that way I can inflict more damage. Floris favours the long sword, while Suelyn is adept with bow and arrow. Suelyn is lady number three, she is small-boned, coffee-coloured like me and more gentle than Floris and I, but she would never let any harm come to our Lord and Master. Zannard calls her his anchor.

After the battle is done, Floris and I often fight with each other to be first to bed Zannard.

It is something to behold to be with him after battle; the energy is so strong and he makes love so passionately. Sometimes he will force us apart and takes one of us to lie with him, while the other fumes, but just lately, I notice that he often slips quietly away and lies with Suelyn who gentles him and then he relaxes and rests well. On awaking, he taunts Floris and I, on what we have missed! The truth of the matter is that I know Floris plots to kill me, just as I plan to do the same to her. Suelyn is no threat to either of us, she is kind and gentle and does so much good for Zannard, she has no harm in her at all.

Floris and I are too alike, we both want Zannard the same way. We watch each other and wait. For all the hate, love and passion between us, we both endeavour not to let it get in the way of our protection of Zannard. We are a fierce-looking pair, covered in scars from sword cuts. I am missing my left nipple, cut off in the heat of battle, the man that did that to me is missing much more! Floris is missing an ear and two fingers on her left hand. Zannard says we scare the living daylights out of the enemy with just the way we look. We are women of the fiercest type, it doesn't matter how battle-scarred we are, Zannard loves us both passionately. The point being, neither Floris nor I want to share this man of ours, each of us wants him for herself.

Apparently, the trouble between Floris and myself is causing quite a problem to the higher archaic. This is our third reincarnation of this particular grouping; I know this is so as I have some memories of these different lives. Floris and I always manage to kill each other one way or another so that one of us is left behind with Zannard. We never get to complete the tasks that have to be done in these lifetimes. Because of our behaviour, we keep having to be reborn to do it all again, until we learn.

It causes so many problems with the Elders of the High council. Lots of planning and work goes into us having to be reborn again and again, to achieve what is required.

It has been already thousands of planet years trying to achieve what should be, what should have been attained in one lifetime. The fact is that the Elders are about to have a very special meeting about how to resolve the problem of Floris and myself. This is unknown, normally these meetings only really happen after the lives are over. This fact alone should frighten us into obedience. This is so scary, but not scary enough to stop both of us trying to get a life alone with Zannard on our own. Although I do know that Floris had one of those recently for some reason or another. I must admit to myself I was half willing to try and get on, but when I realised what Floris was plotting, that thought just faded away.

So we forget what we should be doing and I am planning a new poison. I have heard it is odour free and flavourless. A local woman here, where our camp is now settled, has many salves for our wounds and a lot of secret knowledge of medicines and poisons of a secret culture of long ago.

Our latest battles over and won, we have returned to our tents, the servants lay out clean clothes, food and wine. The four of us bathe together, laughing, playing and relaxing. The clean water washes our wounds and then they are dressed by our local woman!

Yet, I know, under the surface, Floris is planning her next moves, the same as I am.

Just have to make sure my moves come first and those are done in such a way that I look innocent. No more quick thrust with a sword, it is a new game now. A new way to dispose of Floris that leaves me in the clear.

That night, Zannard chooses me to lay with him. No rest for us tonight. We quench our passion for one another and then when we think we are sated, we start all over again. Zannard is very large and he fills me completely. All my senses are heightened and I feel whole. When he withdraws,

I feel the absence of him greatly, inside a great void. So I need him to fill me again and again until I can take no more, then when he does withdraw, I still feel his presence within me and that feeling stays with me for a long while. In some ways, it never fades.

Zannard does not fall asleep until dawn and I, though tired, cannot sleep. I wonder what Floris has been plotting this very night. I know she would have not been able to sleep because of all the noise Zannard and I were making. I also know that every sound would have been driving her to distraction. Just like it does to me when Floris is with Zannard. I sometimes think she makes as much noise as possible and enjoys doing that, knowing it would make me suffer.

I drift off into an uneasy sleep. My last thought being, I must strike first. Much later, Suelyn wakes me with refreshment, I glance over to where Zannard lay to find that he had already gone and with a flash, I know where he is. Suelyn notices my glance.

"He is with Floris," she says. Instantly my stomach clenches then lurches and I am shot through with jealously. Suelyn continues.

"The Elders have all been called to a meeting this full moon, do be careful, Jasander, they will be watching you both." After a pause Suelyn carries on, "Do not do anything, it is not necessary. Zannard loves us all and he has more than enough love to go around us all."

Suelyn was right, I knew Zannard loved us all. I knew his love for me was mine alone and was separate from his love for the other two. When he laid with Floris or Suelyn, the love for me was still there, still mine. I knew all this, but still, I did not want Floris there. I knew she would never stop trying to get rid of me, so I had to strike first.

The next few days were unusual; we had no battles to fight, and hence had much time for ourselves. We rode hard races into the dessert, yelling as we went. Inventing new challenges, changing horses with each other as we rode. Picking stones up off the dessert ground by any means we could devise. We fought mock battles with each other, fooling around till we could laugh no more. In the evenings, the fires were lit and we ate goat dipped in sauces under the stars. As we tasted sweet figs soaked in wine with the syrup dripping down our faces and with the musicians playing such lively and stirring music, it all seemed out of time and place, as if we could all go on forever. Unreal like a dream. Through it all, I felt as if a thousand eyes were watching us all.

We had nights of great lovemaking, it was all something else. I visited the heavens and never wanted to leave, so very slowly I drifted back down to earth, a thousand times or more back into the arms of Zannard.

One night, Zannard took all three of us together to lie with him. Loving each one of us gently, but with strength. We were a unit and the love between us all was so strong, powerful and magnificent that night. Even then I caught Floris looking at me and I knew she was still planning something. I had at that very moment thought perhaps we could make it this time, but I knew with that look from Floris that it was hopeless.

There was to be a banquet. I will make my move then. It was to be our last night here, for tomorrow we pack our tents and will move south to prepare for another battle. If I had my way, there would be one less to pack for. All our new slaves and local women were to serve food with our own servants, so it could be anyone to poison Floris that night. They could not possibly say it was me!

The night was clear and not too hot. Zannard and I had made love all that afternoon. He told me over and over again how much I meant to him and his love for others did not detract anything away from his love for me, that was mine and mine alone. I had never felt so loved and needed in such depth before. It seemed, somehow, like a sort of climax. Like I had no control over what was to come next.

We strode into the big tent in our battle positions. Zannard with Floris and I on either side and Suelyn walking behind. Marched up to the far end of the tent to a rapturous welcome and sat where the cushions were piled high on the raised platform. We seated ourselves in full view of everyone so that all could see their Lord, overall chief of all the tribes. I burst with such pride, for he is my lord and master and my great love, Zannard.

All the music that was playing had stopped until we lowered ourselves onto the cushions and as we sat, a great roar filled the tent, as all the men stood and raised their beakers for a toast of respect and admiration for Zannard.

Zannard acknowledged his men and gestured for everyone to sit.

The banquet began. Long streams of serving girls brought dish after dish of the most delightful food. Then I saw the local woman approaching us with a tray of beakers.

She was bringing our wine.

Suelyn leaned over me.

"I have something very important to tell you," she said and I watched her face as she imparted her news to me. With the local woman's beakers placed in front of us, Zannard reached out and picked his up, smiling into my eyes said, "Remember," he said and drunk deep.

I picked up my beaker and turned to Floris and as she reached for hers, I knocked it over before her hand had even touched it. I shrugged at her and smiled. Then, drunk deeply, of my wine.

Suelyn turned to Floris to tell her the news she had just told me. I saw Floris's face flush and she put out her hand to stop me drinking, too late, I had drunk it all. Of course, Floris had spoken to the same local woman as I had, gained the same knowledge as I had. The same poison that was in my beaker was the same poison that was in Floris beaker. I felt my legs going numb, as it spread up my body quite rapidly to my arms and as I dropped my beaker, I turned and saw the smile on Zannard's face turn to an expression of horror. As the poison touched my heart, I slipped down into darkness.

Floris had won or had she? What Suelyn had whispered to both Floris and Jasander was that when the elders had their meeting earlier that day, a new law had been passed. Whenever Floris or Jasander died by natural causes or foul means or in battle. The other one would be put to death immediately.

The consequences of this law was that both Floris and Jasander would have to protect each other in all other lives to come.

Somewhere in my darkness, I am sure I heard Zannard's laughter.

Chapter 14

Mosstle was waiting in the Hall of Endeavour, eagerly waiting for the return of Zude; he wanted to be the first to greet him, for he knew how disappointed he was by a failure of another life. Like himself, he knew that Zude would be worried about the Elder's reaction to another life cut short by his troublesome pair. Now a new law was in place, it should certainly make a difference. Mosstle chuckled to himself at that very thought.

"Zude, welcome back so good to see you, even though I didn't expect you quite so soon."

The two embraced and thumped each other on the back, laughing together at Mosstle's thoughts, Zude had picked that up as he came through the ring.

"Seriously though," said Zude, "I wonder what the elders will make of this last event."

"I think that if that law had been made a few hours earlier, none of this would have happened. After all, Jacelet knocked Flute's beaker over when she knew."

"Well, my friend we must wait and see."

Zude flung his arm around his friend. "Are the girls back yet?"

"Yes, and they are resting. I think both are in shock! Come let us go and find Reed. I know she is keen to see you."

"Where is she?"

"She went to the pools of vitality."

"Just what I need; let's go."

Jacelet and Flute were awake but still being kept in the recovery suite.

"I am so sorry, Jacelet," Flute stood and hugged Jacelet. "If only they would let us have more conscious memory, I am sure it would be different."

"It will be different because we will have to protect each other," laughed Jacelet.

The keeper of the rooms came over to the girls.

"More rest please and no more talking. Into the pods; now girls and I will attend to you both later on when you have completed processing."

Jacelet and Flute grinned at each other as the keeper hurried them along and into the violet haze of the pod chamber.

The Elders were having a pre-meeting confab, as what they wanted to discuss needed to be straight before they made any grand declaration; so no one else was allowed anywhere near the chamber.

"Why have they kept us out?"

"I hope this doesn't mean bad news."

Zude replied, "I just don't know."

The news was out. No grand meeting, the Elders had settled on a majority decision.

The simple fact of Jacelet knocking the poison over when she heard the news swung the vote to keep going. So, after a short rest break, they will begin another reincarnation.

Zamoth and his two sisters, Fukayna and Jakhat, were playing by the edge of the Nile, teasing their cousin mercilessly, daring her to the edge into the water to defy the crocodiles.

Sekhet, in tears over her cousins' teasing, ran off to the safety of her Ipu, who immediately picked her up and comforted her.

"Do not take any notice of your cousins; they are only mad because you are more pretty than them. Time to go, your mother is asking for you."

Zamoth watched as Sekhet ran off. Mad at her, he turned and pushed his sisters into the water. Then ran off as well, as he knew he would be in trouble. His uncle, Xedmose was watching from the high platform and tutted to himself, but taking great note of Zamoth's reaction to his daughter, Sekhet.

Rashida arrived on the scene to gather her charges, but found only the sisters soaking wet, "Just wait till I find your brother."

"You can't do anything because he is going to be the next Pharaoh."

Both girls then ran off, giggling, in the direction of the palace. Meanwhile, a sulking Zamoth was to be found, hiding, in the bulrushes. They shouldn't treat him with disrespect. After all, he was to be Pharaoh one day and then he had to marry his sisters. Secretly, he would rather marry his cousin, but he knew that they had to keep the bloodline pure. Maybe he would persuade his uncle to let him take Sekhat as a third wife.

Zamoth was growing fast and with his growth came memories, bit by bit, of other lives and strange memories. He had kept this all to himself, some instinct inside him knew this was the best thing to do. He was to be the God/Pharaoh one day and knew he had to have all his wits about him. So all that was slowly unfolding to him, was for him only and meanwhile he would act a boy of his own age would.

A few moons later, Zamoth was down amongst the bulrushes with his sisters.

There were playing 'when I am Pharaoh' and the two girls were pretending to serve him with refreshments. Laughing and giggling through it all.

Zamoth suddenly became serious, "When you are both women, I will marry you both, but now I want to see yours and you will see mine, but not to touch it unless I say."

Slowly, Zamoth pulled his clothing aside and handled his phallus, showing the girls.

"Well," he said, "I am waiting."

Jakhart pulled her clothing to one side and showed what she had; giggling, Fukayna followed suit.

"No giggling, this is serious, I have to know. Open yourselves up so I can see inside," Zamoth ordered.

Zamoth knelt to look closer.

"It looks like you have little phalluses as well. Stand still both of you," he ordered.

Zamoth touched the bud of one girl, then the other.

Then with a thumb on each girl, he circled, then rubbed each bud making then both squeak, with half pleasure, half fear, but curious for more. His eyes met Jakhart's for a moment and they were back in another life, another time. The recognition faded from Jakhart as she looked at his phallus and squirming said, "It's growing, will it burst?"

Rashida's voice, calling out over the river for them, made them jump. Pulling all clothing back in place, Zamoth said, "This is our secret, no one must know."

As the three made their way out of the bulrushes, another pair of eyes watched them leave. Only then, would Sekhet allow herself to touch herself, the same way Zamoth had touched her cousins, again and again.

It was the day of the grand joining. The last moon the two sisters had bled, although they were still very young. Uncle Xedmose had announced the fact, even though, the Pharaoh and the children's mother were still so far away in Ethiopia. He was so used to being Regent while his brother was away, that sometimes he forgot he was not the Pharaoh. After all, they had been gone for over two years. So he had taken the decision to allow the priests to join the brother and sisters as one. Zamoth protested that they should wait till their parents returned, but when Uncle said it must be done, Zamoth protested no more, as he was very eager to conjoin with his sisters. More memories had made him impatient. Impatient to be a proper man, instead of just their secret touching and exploring.

What the children didn't know was that Uncle Xedmose had already put into motion plans that would ensure that the Pharaoh and his wife would never return. Xedmose intended to remain in control, some way or the other. He wasn't ready to relinquish any of the power. Not now, not ever.

The day of the priests joining ceremony dawned hot; hardly a breath of wind and feeling of heaviness was in the air. The sisters were restless, they knew what to expect and knew what Zamoth wanted from them, but they were restless; Jakhat missed their mother. She had been gone so long and her parents should be here, for today of all days. Fukayna neither liked nor trusted her uncle, she didn't like the way he looked at her or her sister. Zamoth knew Uncle was up to something, but not sure what and being keen to have the ceremony done, he ignored all other feelings.

After all, his slowly dawning consciousness was bringing him memories of fighting, conflict, betrayal, responsibility, expansion and marvellous times with his chosen women, but being of an age when the throbbing of increased sexual power drove him, it was far more important to him to release his frustration and explore all that his mind unfolded to him sexually, that the rest of his gained knowledge got pushed to the far recesses of his mind.

The priest ceremony came to a close and the slow procession to the long hall for the banquet was well on its way when two warriors burst into the scene wearing the Pharaoh's colours. They staggered into the hall, shouting incoherently all sort of mixed messages.

"They are dead."

"Everyone is dead."

"We are only alive because we didn't drink the water."

"All dead. We are alive because we were on guard and drunk our own water."

"We watched as some rough men checked the dead."

"They didn't know we were there."

"The water hole was poisoned."

"It was safe last year."

"We got away safe."

"Got here as quick as we could."

"We were coming for the ceremony."

"I am sure we were followed."

"I thought I knew one of the men."

Uncle Xedmose took charge, shouting orders over the warriors' disjointed words.

"Take them away, give them food and drink, baths and clean clothes."

"What was that all about," Zamoth pushed himself forward.

"What was happening and who is dead? They were wearing my father's colours."

"It's all being sorted," said Xedmose calmly. "You go back to enjoying the feast and your bedding."

At those words, Zamoth turned eagerly back to his wives.

Zamoth's bedding was all he hoped it would be and for his sisters, now his wives they just could not get enough of him. All Zamoth's memories of his art of lovemaking came flooding back to him and he surprised himself of what he was able to achieve, because of the love between the sisters, he could bed them together and he saw that as long as he treated them equally, there was little jealousy or resentment between them. So as the art of lovemaking flooded back through his mind, he saw that the two sisters had been his to love through many lifetimes. This alone gave him much power and he was able to be erect for a long time and could take each sister many times in many ways. When his phallus finally settled in repose, he had both the sisters laying on their backs with their legs well open. He looked at their openings, seeing with some satisfaction that they showed signs of being well used. He lay between the girls and first with one, then the other, sucked and bit their buds, then lapped all around causing them to shriek with delight, begging for more.

Promising his girls more pleasure still to come, they finally fell asleep. So it was no surprise that the sun was high in the sky before the three of them even stirred.

After baths and refreshment, the three eagerly tumbled back into bed for more sexual adventures without a thought given to yesterday's events with the Pharaoh's men. Of course, this was what Xedmose wanted while he sorted and arranged everything the way he wanted. So, by the time the trio emerged, sore in places and well sated, ready to go into court life. Xedmose had it all planned. When Zamoth finally asked his uncle what had happened to his father's men, he was shocked to the core by his uncle's answer.

Apparently, his father and mother were hurrying back for the joining ceremony and had stopped over at a well-known watering hole, but it seems at some time someone had it poisoned. So overnight everyone died except the ones on guard duty.

They had hurried back to tell of the disaster, but they must have had some of the water after all, because they all died in the night before the full tale could be told.

Xedmose then added that his men had already set off to collect the Pharaoh's body and his wife. So it was all sorted, he would personally take charge of all events until, Zamoth was feeling better and more settled into the joining. There was no hurry.

After the first shock had passed, then all the doubts he had about the death and how Xedmose had handled everything, slowly dissolved. The grand funeral and internment in his parents' pyramid came and went. Zamoth began to think it was time for him to take his rightful place as Pharaoh. Both his wives were with child and so his thoughts turned to the country and his inheritance. So Zamoth approached his uncle about him relinquishing the regency and planning a grand ceremony to pronounce Zamoth as Pharaoh.

Xedmose had other ideas. He presented the idea to Zamoth that he should take Sekhet his daughter, as his third wife, to strengthen and promote the bloodline, making the dynasty even stronger.

It hardly took a moment for Zamoth to agree, he had always yearned after his cousin since they were children, and all the acts he did with his sister wives, he could try with Sekhat, especially since his wives were both with child and he was having to be more careful.

Xedmose added that he could manage to stay on, as regent, so that it would give them time for Sekhet to settle well into his life!

So Sekhet was joined to Zamoth, in a quieter ceremony, but with epic bedding.

Sekhet was shy, to begin with, not wanting Zamoth to look at her, but he was patient.

Carefully disrobing her, touching her slowly, arousing her almost without her noticing. He delighted in her love bud which was a small pebble and matched her small nipples, her delicacy delighted him. When fully aroused and ready for him, she amazed him by throwing aside all inhibitions and responding with fierce passion.

They soon became so enamoured of each other, that they never noticed how they upset the sister wives or the state of court and country. Xedmose made himself Pharaoh, in all but name, acting as chief priest and divine intermediary for all of Egypt. All this went over Zamoth's head.

His two sister-wives were both delivered of lusty baby boys within days of each other, this almost passed unnoticed, but a thought flitted into Zamoth's brain that he now had the beginnings of his own dynasty and he should start to look outward and onwards to the future.

It dawned on him that he hadn't seen his uncle for a long time, nor any of the council.

None of them ever came to him about any decisions they all made and with a growing horror, he realised he knew nothing at all about the state, about the results of his parent's death. Worse of all, he had neglected his first wives, whom he loved dearly, realising his lust for Sekhet had run away with him. Also, all his old servants seemed to have been replaced with Xedmose's people. He began to realise he had been made a fool, playing right into his uncle's hands. Well, he was not going to be a puppet Pharaoh, but he needed the help of his sister-wives, but not Sekhet, just in case she had known what her father was up to. Though Zamoth hoped she might be just an innocent party to any of this, but had to tread slowly first.

He headed off to his sister-wives' quarters, eager suddenly to see his two sons and to see his wives as well. With a rush of tenderness and desire, he hurried along through the corridors to be with his sister-wives.

The reunion was emotional, how could he have neglected what he had with them. He took both of them to bed and loved them well into the late afternoon. He realised that sharing was the way forward. After spending time with his sons, loving every moment, amazed at their smallness and how alike they were; they could be brothers instead of cousins. He then sat down with his sister-wives and poured out all his horror of how he neglected them. How his mind was so troubled when he had come to realise what his uncle had done, how ashamed he was that he had allowed it all to happen.

Jakhat and Fukayna listened intently, then Jakhat said, "We came many times to see you but were turned away by the guards, they said you didn't want to be disturbed."

"I said no such thing."

But hung his head as he thought he probably would have not have been bothered.

"Uncle was keeping us from you," Fukayna said in anger.

"How are we going to deal with him," asked Jakhat.

They talked throughout the night and when morning came Zamoth left to go back to Sekhet. He had to carry on as usual, he really wanted to see if he could tell if Sekhat knew anything of her father's plans. Meanwhile, his two sister-wives were going to sort out who, amongst them all would be on their side.

Zamoth was so disappointed, there was so few that wanted him to be Pharaoh. On the good side was the fact that those on his side were good men, well known for their good judgement and had backed Zamoth's father. Many of them thought that Xedmose had something to do with the old Pharaoh's death and didn't like the way he had taken over everything. A lot of Xedmose's army were paid mercenary men and probably could be paid to change sides, but if they changed once, they could change again. Instead of a blood bath battle, Zamoth's wise advisors wanted to have a council with Xedmose's advisors. Just trying to organise this was such a nightmare that Zamoth despaired, thinking a terrible battle was the only way or a splitting of the kingdom which also was unthinkable.

His one light was that Sekhat was seemingly innocent about all her father's plans.

Most upset about being on the opposite side to him, to the point where Zamoth thought it best not to tell her all their plans.

Many moons passed with endless talk, with one side then another disagreeing on any solution. Then Xedmose came up with his solutions. Realising that his health was failing a little, and not wanting his bloodline to disappear, came up with his idea.

He wanted his daughter Sekhet to be made Great Royal wife. Her son to be made next Pharaoh after Zamoth. The sister-wives to be downgraded to minor wives with little chance of their sons being made Pharaoh. In exchange for this idea, Xedmose would stand down and let Zamoth be Pharaoh and God King.

Sekhel who had denied knowing any of her father's ideas was shocked and but secretly quite pleased at the idea.

The sister-wives, well, they were horrified.

The councils sat in a closed meeting. Everyone waited.

It was all done. Zamoth had been crowned Pharaoh and God/King with Sekhel at his side as Great Royal Wife. His sister-wives were not made minor wives but principal wives two and three. It was a horrible blow to the sisters, but Zamoth insisted that they were still part of the inner Royal Family. He hoped dearly that they could all get on well together, as he loved all of them dearly. He loved his sons and at the moment there was no sign of Sekhet being with child. Xedmose was being allowed to stay in the palace with no official role except a new one created for him as Father of Pharaoh's wife. It was an empty role, but it kept everyone happy! Almost.

Zamoth had the sister-wives moved to a wing nearer his with Sekhat. He had ideas of all being together but realised that would not work. That would be one step too far as the sister-wives were anti-Sekhat, not openly but he felt it in the ether.

So he was strolling into the sister-wives' wing when he found them in bed together, that shook him for a moment, but he quickly acknowledged that since when he was with them, they were all in bed together, so why not when he was not. He found to his surprise that he liked the thought because it stirred in him a different kind of sexual feeling, but with that feeling came the sudden insight of the two wives, always at odds with one another, always killing each other, to be the only one left to be with him.

Then the swift knowledge of a new law, that if one dies the other does too. Stunned, he watched the wives, wondering what was so different in this lifetime to make them so close, like one unit. Being so aroused with a different type of energy, he leapt onto the bed, making the wives squeal with delight. Lying on his back, he pulled one wife astride his loins and the other astride his face.

Later that day, he sat and recounted what he had remembered of the law and knowledge of his sister-wives to Sekhet, thinking she would be as fascinated by this knowledge, as he was. Feeling a little putout, she listened, but within a few moments was lost in a new energised feeling as Zamoth rode her intently and deeply.

The years passed in a good way for Zamoth, he learned to control his sexual energy, so he ruled it and not the other way around, knowing his growing wisdom and judgement was making him a good Pharaoh and acknowledging that must come first. His sister-wives continued to be close with each other and produced more children, but the downside was Sekhet, she took a long time to get with child, but then seem to lose them before they had a good hold in her womb. So it was Sekhet, that was envious of the sister's children and didn't like to be around them. After ailing for a long while, her father finally passed on, but Sekhet knew he was bitterly disappointed in her, that she had not produced the live heir he so desired to carry on his blood.

Finally, when all hope had gone, Sekhet almost past childbearing years, produced a healthy live boy. He was small but made up for that by being very vocal. Sekhet named him Zamoth. For, he was to be, Pharaoh Zamoth the second. Nobody was allowed to forget that. Young Zamoth was protected, nurtured, spoilt, but whatever care, he remained delicate in the body. Sekhet felt threatened by the healthy boisterous offspring of the sister-wives and wanted them all removed, to another palace. Well away from her beloved son. Zamoth's reaction was almost violent, no way were his sister-wives and his children he adored going to be moved anywhere. He wanted them close. Truth be told, Zamoth had realised his sister-wives and his rowdy offspring meant so much more to him, than his up and down life with Sekhet and she, disturbed by his reaction, knew she had to keep her reactions and feelings to herself.

But she thought, there had to be a way, and a way she would find.

Arrangements were being made for the sisters and Zamoth to visit the watering hole where their parents had died. They wanted to look into what had happened, as it was many years since the murder. Increasingly, Zamoth was becoming more aware of how his uncle manipulated him and had fed him such tales of what had happened. Nothing had been proven, but he remembered the rumours that went around that his uncle had done something.

Sitting around the campfire they talked.

"What if it is too long ago and there is no evidence left."

"The water is pure again."

"Perhaps we should look where the men's bodies are buried."

"Is there no one left alive that remembers?"

"So many people travel this way, use this watering hole. Someone must know."

The three of them talked far into the night.

The next day the soldiers, very reluctantly and not wanting to disturb the dead, shifted through the burial pit of the poisoned men and women of Zamoth's father's court. They found amongst the dead, two members of Xedmose's army in full regalia.

"They could have died doing the burial duty."

"This is not proof that they were here before the killing."

"If they were doing burial duty, why are they dead and why are they at the bottom of the pit."

"Too many unanswered questions."

Zamoth and his sister-wives still had many questions.

The activity around the watering hole was causing interest amongst regular users, and one of the regular users asked to see Zamoth.

He was passing through that night and came across a load of men wearing Xedmose Regalia. He was warned off, to keep away, as the Pharaoh was coming that way. So taking some water, he passed on by. As he went, he was surprised to see

Xedmose's men leaving as well. When he passed again and was warned that the water had gone bad as the Pharaoh and his court had died there from the result of poisoned water.

Well, as far as he was concerned, that was all the proof Zamoth wanted, it confirmed his worst fears. How much had he been manipulated and deceived by his uncle? He ordered that his remains be brought out of his Pyramid and his body left out in the desert for the vultures to devour, so that it could not be used for his uncle's heavenly journey. All his funeral goods to be either destroyed, but those metals of value were melted down for reuse. All record of him destroyed. Sekhet was devastated but Zamoth was adamant.

From that day on, Zamoth spent less and less time in Sekhet rooms and took greater pleasure being with his sister-wives. The last straw to Sekhet was when Zamoth announced he was changing the order of succession. Making the sister-wives' offspring first in line for being Pharaoh. Sekhet remembered something Zamoth had once said and suddenly, the way she had been searching for became clear in her mind.

Jakhat was ill; she just seemed to be fading slowly before their eyes. Zamoth summoned every wise medicine man in the land, offering money and gifts to any that could find a cure. Fukanya was distraught, nursing her sister with devotion. Sekhet took her turn with helping with Jakhat and her children. She was often there all night, helping where she could. Sekhet remarked to Zamoth how she thought Fukanya was so marvellous, insisting on always feeding Jakhat, encouraging her to eat a variety of different dishes. For all that care, Jakhat just faded slowly away. Nothing anyone did ever seemed to help. Fukanya and Zamoth were so distraught. Sekhet was always respectful, always full of admiration for the way Fukanya always found a way to try and make the food appetizing.

One day, when Fukanya was preparing something tasty, Zamoth walked in.

"Sekhet said I should come and help you. What can I do?"

"I need some mild spice. It is not in its usual spot. Could you have a look?"

Fukanya busied herself with the tasty dish of fish she was preparing.

"I can do without; it is not to be found."

She turned when she heard Zamoth gasp, "What is this?"

Zamoth was waving his hands in the air shouting at her.

"What is this, what have you done? Why? How could you! I thought it was all different now."

She couldn't understand what was going on.

"Guards, Guards to me," Zamoth was shouting. Fukanya couldn't understand what was going on, she put her hand out to steady herself. What was the matter?

"Take her away, out of my sight. Put her in the darkest room. Double the guard. No one to see her. No one to give her any water or food. Take her away. Treat her roughly. Take her now."

Fukanya stumbled and the guards just grabbed her, pulled her along by her hair. She screamed, "What have I done? Zamoth, Zamoth."

Even with the poison known, it was too late to reverse the effects, far too late to save Jakhat. Zamoth was shocked, couldn't believe what his sister-wife had done.

Reverting back to type, like the many past lifetimes. He had thought this lifetime it was so different. Jakhat seemed to fret at her sister's absence and she fell into a deep sleep, never to awake from it. Zamoth was gutted. She was to have a grand funeral using the pyramid that Zamoth had built for himself. Fukanya was to be buried alive in the same pyramid. All this time Sekhet was jubilant but hid it so well, always being on hand to help. Sekhet showed all the compassion and understanding Zamoth seemed to need so badly, she was always by his side expressing shock at what had happened.

Zamoth began to rely on her for many things and began to need her more and more.

The day of the grand funeral arrived. Jakhat was laid to rest in her beautifully painted sarcophagus, dressed beautifully in all the regalia of her rank and all the goods needed for her journey into eternity. Fukanya was laid in an open type coffin beside her sister, restrained but alive, in just a plain funeral cloth covering her. She was to be her sister's slave on the eternal journey. As the chambers closed, you could hear Fukanya screaming until the last stone was placed and then you could hear her no more.

Sekhet took her place at Zamoth's side, respectfully, sorrowfully and supportive and at her side, stood Zamoth the second the heir apparent, her son and the next Pharaoh, and if her next plan went well, that would not be too long in coming.

Chapter 15

"That was certainly a lifetime with a difference, always they have been centred on Jacelet and Flute. This was more for you, Zude, a bit of a surprise for you, and all with a limited life consciousness."

Mosstle and Zude shook hands and hugged.

"And," Mosstle continued, "learning control over your massive energy source in a human lifetime and what about Sekhet! Who would have thought she had it in her."

"Yes, she is always so quiet and calm in other lives."

"Well, it just shows you, you had no idea that she planned it all."

"No, never occurred to me."

"In our own worlds and universes we are just our own true selves, but in this one, you had personalities and lack of consciousness to deal with. No wonder it is so hard for all concerned."

Mosstle pondered a moment, "Well, it looks like you have three spirited ladies now and I can't wait to see what happens next. Come, let us find Reed and celebrate your return."

"I believe Danka is back from her world, let's find her as well."

"And your ladies, we all deserve a real get together and be ourselves. Come, let's go."

Feeling lighter, the two friends sent their thoughts out to the others and with arms around each other thought themselves to the rendezvous. It would be a pleasant interlude before the summons for the grand meeting.

It was one of the biggest gatherings for a long time. It seemed that everyone wanted to hear about what was to come next. The pews were filled to bursting point and if you looked up at the tiers, they were full of entities as far as you could see. None of them had any idea what was in line for the group and the eager anticipation hummed in the air.

The Wise One appeared, his long hair and beard materialising first, so light and bright that it resulted in everyone covering their eyes. Then after a pause, the rest of him was there, toned down so it no longer pained their sight.

It was unfolded to the gathering that Zude was to take two personalities running concurrently, on opposing sides. With him, his three ladies, also Reed, Anka and Xatar, spilt between the two sides.

The buzz in the arena was electric, all communicating in various methods. Thoughts so powerful you could see them as wisps of cloud floating along and gathering in ever-growing thought-forms above all.

Zude was blown away. Immediately, a thought from the wise one filled his mind with a powerful energy. Making it clear he was quite capable and advanced enough to fulfil this well. Mosstle picking up on this said, "I will help in every way I can from this level. You have my lady with you, so what more could you want."

Zude laughed and thanked his friend.

Zachariah and Faith.

We were poor, but then most of the people around here are poor, food was hard to come by. The ground scorched by the sun had brought forth no good crops, even the birds had disappeared because the people had been eating them; it was the only meat they could find. Lizards and snakes had also long since disappeared.

Zachariah had said, "Anything to keep body and soul alive."

I had returned home empty-handed, as I could find nothing to buy or scavenge. Only a few grains in the pot and they would not go far with five to feed.

Zachariah is my husband of many years, a good man, who leads our people to the best of his ability. Zachariah's two sisters, Hannah and Sarah, never married. There is a shortage of unmarried men in our tribe; too many have left to find a better way of living or have died while fighting for our freedom. Hannah and Sarah did not want to find husbands outside the tribe. Zachariah's mother, Ruth, is a wise woman, treated with respect by our tribe. Unusual, because women are always second place in our world.

My name is Faith. I was the mother of three boys and the last plague took all three in as many days and I have no heart to have any more to bring into this world that's harsh and dry. Better that they are not born. Zachariah's mind is with the people, on how to get better conditions for them and not on me. So, no fear of any more children. Zachariah talks often now, about a new man from another place who is so keen to help. His name is Yeshua. Zachariah thinks that with his help it will strengthen us.

Zavier and Josephina

I am so bored. Zavier is out with his men, seeking the Jewish rebels. Astria and Lydia my two body servants make sure I have everything I need. I am good to them for they have been with me since childhood and my father gifted them to me when Zavier took me as his wife. Not all the centurion's wives are kind to their slaves, but I value mine. I have everything I could possibly need to live my life of luxury, but I get so bored of drink and food, gambling and parties. I want something more out of life. I hate the rebels, they take my Zavier away from me when he should be here paying me attention. We have such a good coupling; there is no one like him. When I first saw him, I knew he was the one for me. He had been away for many years fighting battles, gaining new territory for the emperor and empire. Bringing back with him, many slaves and many riches and wonders from faraway places. He is much older than me, but I knew there was no one else for me. I love him to bits but I do wish he was here with me more. I am aware that sometimes he thinks I am childish and have been spoilt by my father, but I know he loves me deeply, so he tolerates my silly ways.

Zachariah and Faith

Zachariah has called a meeting for tonight, all will attend. When Zachariah calls a meeting all the tribe will come, such is the deep respect that they all have for him. I, with the women that are allowed to attend, will stand at the back of the room. We have our opinions, but what with the men stating theirs, ours are often not heard at all.

My mind is with Zachariah anyway. We think the same thoughts strongly.

All the coin we do have seems to go to the Romans as payments. To enable us to live, to leave us alone, to have water. I used to collect water every day, morning and evening when it was free, but now a tax is on the water and I can only afford to collect every other day. As well as hunger, we are thirsty, which is worse. They like to control our every movement, there is a levy to leave the city and another to return. There is a levy to cross the square and it seems that there is a guard on every street corner. I think the guards put the coin they charge into their own pocket, to buy more wine.

They like to be constantly drunk, because they hate our land. If they all hate being here, why do they stay? The Romans are forbidden to touch our women because we are so 'dirty'. We are supposed to carry dreadful diseases that could infect the Roman army, 'God forbid'. So they are forbidden bodily contact. I think it is the Romans that have brought the dreadful diseases with them, but they like to blame everyone else. I know that they do not like it here; they call it a godforsaken country. We know different, before the Romans, we called it god blessed.

All meetings are forbidden. No more than three men may stand and talk at any time; so tonight's meeting is full of danger. There is a curfew at sunset, so we have to pass through the streets in the dark without torches, but that is not a problem as there is no oil for the torches anyway!

Zavier and Josphina

Zavier moved cautiously through the streets. It seemed to me that a thousand eyes were watching my every move; I shivered, then quickly turned to see if my men had noticed. Battles I could handle, but this, trying to control a race of people in a bleak land was something else. I hated this round of duty; I knew my men hated it as well. Being here in this dry, arid land, when all I wanted was to be back home. The people here hated us and not so surprisingly when we tried to suppress them at every turn. Xanthus stepped up beside me, placing a reassuring hand on my shoulder and both of us stepped out together with renewed vigour. Zavier's informers had said that there was talk of a meeting tonight and that a new man Yeshua was speaking. They had been watching and following Zachariah for some time, so expected him to lead them.

"Surely you don't mean to go tonight. I could forbid it and have you confined to the house." Josphina was aghast, what if her husband found out?

"I should stop this nonsense at once."

"You could come with me my lady and hear his words."

Josphina, shocked, retorted, "And what if Zavier found out. I couldn't do that."

She took Lydia's hands.

"I don't want to know anything about it. If you get caught it is on your own head and you do not mention who you are or where you live. It is too dangerous for us all."

"My lady, I have arranged to stay with a friend tonight after the meeting and do not worry. I would never betray you or your family."

With those final words, Lydia slipped out of the door.

Josphina turned to Astria, "Make sure her absence is not noticed." And swept out of the room.

Josphina was relieved in some way, that Zavier was not at home that night, but she was sure he would be involved in finding the secret meeting. What was it that this man called

Yeshua had that caused Lydia to dare to go to hear his words? Quiet and gentle Lydia, who, she had known all of her life.

Zachariah and Faith

Zachariah does not want me to go tonight, he says it is far too dangerous, he knows that he has been watched and often followed. He wants me to stay with his mother, Ruth, for she always goes to hear him speak; he wants me to make sure that she doesn't leave the house for she is weak now and I think death will come for her soon. I think death will come for us all soon. If starvation doesn't get us first, the Romans will.

After Zachariah has left with his friends, I will slip out in the dark and go to hear the words that will be spoken. I will go first, to talk with Mother Ruth, for she has been our mainstay over the years. With her strong spirit and her beliefs, she has often shown us all the way forward. I know that Sarah and Hannah wanted to go, but they are more likely to do as Zachariah asks. It is important that someone stays with Mother; now that the end is getting nearer, I do not want her to be alone – she means so much to us all.

"The good lord will take me when he is ready, so I want you all to go and tell me everything when you return."

"No, we cannot leave you alone, I would be so worried. I will stay."

"No, Faith, you must go. I need you to keep watch over my son. If someone must stay, let it be Hannah. Now go."

The house is full of men, all ready to slip out into the darkness, they came to protect Zachariah; making sure he gets to the meeting safely. I know a similar group is guarding Yeshua. I can hardly wait to meet this man. It is to be held in the cellars of the wine merchant's house. The wine merchant says as he has no wine anymore, he has plenty of room for all of the men. I take a large dark wrap in for my husband and wrap him well, covering his face. I want him back, this man of mine, so I put many good thoughts into my careful wrapping. I hope this will keep him safe in the dark.

We look deeply into each other's eyes, no need for words, we know each other's thoughts well. With a quiet movement, they are suddenly all gone. The room seems big with their absence, so much space. Moving into the next room to check on Zachariah's mother, I find her sleeping well, with Hannah sitting so still beside her, holding on so tightly to Mother's hand. We look at each other, I too, when I sit with Mother hold on to her hand for dear life. As if we could stop her leaving us. Sarah appears, wrapped in her cloak, and we slip out in the dark together.

Zavier and Josphina

Sitting quietly at the table the two men were planning the night's events.

"The informer said that the meeting was at the wine merchant's house."

"I think that is too obvious and open," Zavier replied pushing his beaker out towards the girl for a refill.

"Could be the informer is feeding us false information."

"We know these people are devious. This meeting is huge, many will be going. Let's just sit here and watch a while. I have placed extra men out there to watch and the word will get back to us quickly."

Xanthus shook his head and placed his hand over the top of his beaker. The girl wandered to the other tables.

Zavier pushed his beaker away and said clearly, "No more wine, men. Tonight I need your heads clear."

Zavier turned to Xanthus.

"You know this business turns my stomach, I am not made for this. As soon as I can, I will return to Rome."

Xanthus nodded, whether in agreement or not, Zavier was not sure.

Meanwhile, Josphina was fretting about Lydia. What was it that this man Yeshua had to say that made her gentle Lydia risk all to hear him? Should she go as well? She was bored with this country and the way Zavier was so tired and always on duty.

Josphina longed to return to Rome and she wondered how Zavier thought about it all.

It possibly would have been better if they had children, but for some reason, they never arrived. It wasn't for lack of offerings to the gods, it seemed that they never favoured them that way for they lacked in nothing else.

Zachariah and Faith

It is so dark in the quiet streets, we are the last to leave for the meeting and I have such a feeling of foreboding. I press it firmly down so that I will not feel the fear.

Sarah and I slide along the streets and alleys, slipping through the shadows. Where are the guards? They seem to have left their posts. I do not like this at all. We reach the wine merchant's house and enter carefully into the cellars. It is empty and the silence rebounds off the walls. Zachariah is clever, he knew I would come and listen, so he told me the wrong meeting place. Trying as ever to protect me, now I am troubled and so is Sarah. How can I warn him about the absence of the guards? There is such a strange feeling in the air. What can I do! Sarah and I stand staring at each other in this empty place, not knowing what to do next. No one to ask, no one to follow; so we both turn and slip back through the streets to go home.

I cannot settle and go out onto the roof and sit in the heavy night air. I am desperately trying to scent the air, some clue to where my man can be, it is all too quiet. Slowly, the creeping dawn touches the edge of the town and from the roof, I can see out into the desert. Dumbfounded, I look at the many tracks in the sand, tracks of many feet passing in the direction of the hills.

"Sarah," tumbling down the steps, I shout out her name, "Sarah."

Zavier and Josphina

Hidden behind the rocks, Zavier and his men observed all the coming and goings, waiting for the meeting to begin. Impatient for Zachariah and Yeshua's turn to speak.

Zavier badly wanted these two men. Then when it is done, he could go home; he was heartily sick of all this cloak and dagger stuff. Inside himself, he had a feeling of what they were doing here in this land was wrong. Very wrong, looking at Xanthus's face, he saw a fleeting expression that his second in command might feel the same way too.

Josphina and her body servant, Astria also watched from the rocks. She was excited and fearful but had to know what was that had Lydia so enthralled. They didn't dare to go down and join the crowds and she knew her Zavier would be here, so they remained hidden from view. Not totally hidden though; one of the Roman guards informed Xanthus about the watching women and Xanthus, after checking, kept the information to himself.

Zachariah's speech was political, hitting hard against the conditions of starvation and poverty that the Romans had caused, but it was Yeshua that stirred something inside him, he preached of a better world in his father's kingdom, it wasn't the words so much as this man's presence that affected him. Watching the crowds, he saw how he had affected them too, a powerful man in his gentle way.

Zavier gave the signal and like an avalanche, the Romans descended on the crowd, cutting down anyone in their way, as they blasted through to reach their targets.

At that moment, two women slid away from the rocks, then fled.

Zachariah and Faith

Sarah comes with me as we hasten out of the town. Through the gates, with no guards, out into the desert following the tracks of many people. Nothing seems right, it is too silent, too empty. We reach the rocks and climb over rough stones and reach an opening. This was where the meeting was held, this is where everyone had been. The signs of a quick departure is everywhere – bits of clothing, pots, ruffled sand and debris. Reddish stains in the ground. Where was everyone now? All these signs of struggle and disruption, but no one to be seen.

Sarah and I return to the town, the guards are back on the gates and we have to pay to enter. The town seemed so normal. Back at home, Hannah was weeping; death had called while we were gone and took Mother Ruth. At least she will be spared all that is going to happen now and where is my husband?

Zavier and Josphina

Such a loud mix of sounds. Zavier's men are jubilant. They have them both. Zachariah and Yeshua. Zachariah was here in town, being held with the remains of his men. The bodies of those slaughtered had been tossed in a heap outside the walls. Zavier knew this would inflame their religious beliefs. The bodies need burial before sundown and it was way past that time. Xanthus was organising extra guards around the garrison and near the dead men. Stopping anyone who tried to claim a body.

Striking them down and adding them to the rotting pile. Dead or alive.

Yeshua had been taken elsewhere, by order of Pilate. Zavier wondered what was going on and he had received orders that Zachariah was to die immediately with the remaining men. Zavier was tired and feeling sick over all the bloodshed, put off his orders and sat alone just watching. He wanted to see Zachariah and Yeshua, he wanted to see and know what it was that these men had. For some inexplicable reason, he was so drawn towards Zachariah. He was so tired, he slipped off into a disturbed sleep.

Zachariah and Faith

The Romans came, it was almost a relief to see them. At last, I would find out the truth and see my Zachariah. We were ordered to go with them. Hannah, Sarah and I.

We were led out of the town walls, past a heap of our men rotting in the sun. Out of the East Gate, which led to the

117

stoning pits. There was my beloved Zachariah, standing with four others. Dear God is that all there is left of our men.

Two Romans stood by the edge of the pit gazing down at the men. One turned and looked at me, then pulled me to the edge.

"You, his wife," pulling at my hair that had escaped my hood. Forcing me to look directly at him.

The other man said, "Leave her be Xanthus."

Who said, "Will you give the order now?"

Looking at Zachariah, Zavier felt such a strange attachment to the man. It was like looking at himself. He just could not give the order.

Xanthus shouted, "Throw, everyone Throw. Death to anyone who does not obey."

Those that refused were either thrown into the pit or cut down where they stood.

The man Xanthus, screamed at me, "Throw."

Slowly, the stones were being thrown at my beloved Zachariah.

"Throw," a guard said, as he threatened me with his sword.

My eyes met Zachariah and he imperceptible nodded at me. Slowly, I picked up a stone, like Hannah and Sarah, threw the stones wide, threw at the space between the men.

"Throw," shouted the guards, and I, sick to my very soul, watched the horror unfold in front of my eyes as I pretended to throw at my beloved. Watched, as he and the others were battered, broken and bloodied. Passers-by were ordered to throw and they did not know my man and threw with a vengeance.

Zavier and Josphina.

Zavier couldn't believe what was happening. Every stone that was thrown at Zachariah he felt, he felt as if part of himself was dying. He locked eyes with Zachariah, in a moment that seemed like years, visions and energy passed between them. I know this man so well, but how. He sensed and felt death creeping over this man and himself. What was it? He felt so ill, that he knew he must leave or he would perish as well.

Lydia was saying:

"Hurry, Hurry. We must see what is happening to him." She was pulling Astria along.

Josphina, who had felt such a compulsion to go, hurried along with them. Why on earth was she doing this? If Zavier ever found out! They tumbled into the Square where so many people were pushing and shoving to see this man Yeshua.

"There he is," screamed Lydia, trying to get closer. What they saw shocked the three.

This gentle spoken man was being flayed before their very eyes.

"Get back, get back. The Roman pushed them back and the three of them tumbled over one another. Trodden on and dishevelled, they pulled back to the edge of the crowd.

"What can we do?" Lydia desperately looked around the crowd for help, seeing none but jeering, terrible people so enjoying the scene. Josphina came to her senses first and pulled the two girls back away from the scene.

"We must go; we must not be seen here."

Zachariah and Faith

Much later, when the guards had left and the sun was sinking fast. We picked up his broken body, misshapen and bloody. We took him home. Bathed him and tried to straighten his limbs. Wrapping him in cloths, sweetened with herbs, all ready for burial. We will bury him in the caves where his mother and our sons lay, as soon as it is day. I was numb, past all desires of life. I just wanted to join Zachariah and my sons.

We laid Zachariah by his mother's side in the caves where my sons are. I had a once in a lifetime love for Zachariah and knew my heart was with him. Hannah and Sarah are preparing to leave the town and asked me to go with them, but all I ever wanted is here in these caves.

I know the Romans will come for me shortly. How will I die, I do not know. I do not fear death, for it is welcome, only the manner with which it will come. I sit ready for them.

Waiting for the moment I can be with my beloved once more and I know he is waiting for me.

Zavier and Josphina

Xanthus reported Zavier's reluctance to give orders over Zachariah's stoning and his strange behaviour afterwards. He also reported how he observed Josphina and her body servants at the gathering. One of the guards also reported pushing Josphina away from Yeshua.

The guard was sent to Zavier's house to arrest all who were there.

Zavier was back at the stoning ground looking for Zachariah's body, he felt this strong compulsion to touch feel and see his body. To stop this feeling of half of himself missing. When one of his loyal men caught up with him and explained what Xanthus had done.

"Where is she?" demanded a demented Zavier.

"The garrison prison."

Zavier rooted to the ground for a moment, shocked, drew his sword and ran back towards the town. He never made it back to the town wall. Xanthus was ready and he appeared, leapt in front of him and savagely struck him down. Zavier cried out as he fell and his last sight was of Zachariah holding his hands out in welcome.

Josphina was crouched in the corner of the jail. When the gates flew open and another woman was roughly thrown on the floor.

"Another one of you, Yeshua's followers to die with you and do not expect your husband to come for you. He is dead."

With laughter, the jailer slammed the door shut.

Josphina crawled over to the other woman. Putting her arms around her, she felt as though she had known this woman forever. Faith raised her eyes, with such deep sadness, looking at Josphina feeling this strange but familiar bond.

Josphina said, "Together, we will face whatever comes with strength."

Chapter 16

Walking backwards and forwards, stamping his feet with impatience, Zude could barely contain himself, glancing every few seconds at the transporting ring.

Laughing heartily at his impatience, Mosstle said:

"They will be here shortly."

No sooner had he said this the ring vibrated rapidly and two figures appeared.

Helping each other out of the ring, they then both threw themselves at Zude who, opening his arms wide with pleasure, embraced them both before all three ended on the ground. Laughing Mosstle helped them all up on their feet, stated, "Well, it seems we have all earned a break from this constant reincarnation. Not a long one, but a break anyway, so let's not waste our time here."

In moments, Zude with Jacelet and Flute vanished. With Mosstle thinking himself also gone, was just a whisker behind.

First of all was some balancing, repair and healing. The three stood on raised dais as coloured energies flooded their beings, erasing the harmful energies from the last life that had clung to their true selves. Renewed, they met Reed, who had returned earlier and with Mosstle, the five of them thought themselves to the sacred pools, to rest, relax and continue to renew themselves for a while.

There, in perfect harmony with the rest of the group, they enjoyed a rare idyllic interlude.

The wise one was in deep thought conversation with the other top Elders. Pleased at some of the growth achieved, sad that they thought it wasn't enough for their liking.

Thought-forms in vivid colours whirled around their heads and filled the room from their different vibrations. After a lot of shaking heads and occasional nods, they came to their decision. The next life was to be the last of this series. If the group did not manage the control of energies in that lifetime experience, the Elders will pull the plug withdrawing all and leaving this particular universe to its slow unfolding or destruction.

"Even though," said the wise one, "I said we couldn't afford to lose another universe if it doesn't happen this lifetime and the group do not manage control. We will pull out as there are plenty of other universes where we can carry on our work."

With those closing words, the group was summoned back from the sacred pools.

To prepare, learn of the undertaking of the next reincarnation.

Zude was to take over a physical already inhabited by an 8-year-old boy and Reed, a 10-year-old girl had been selected, the others to born as new babies. Parents for them already chosen and expecting.

Jade born of elderly parents, was an only child, was thinking how shocked her parents had been when she announced she was taking a gap year from her studies to drive down through Europe, hoping to end up in India. She didn't know why but always felt drawn to the country, and besides, the fact she had received several letters over the past few years from her friend, Flick, who had set off backpacking straight from college after her GCEs at sixteen. Flick came from a large bustling family who encouraged her to get out into the big world and see what it was all about before deciding what she wanted to do.

Jade was thinking about the differences in their family life and their upbringing. How when they were school kids, she had loved going back to Flick's home for tea, to that mad, organised chaos of their home. All seven siblings played a musical instrument and after tea, was practise time, sometimes as a group. Jade would listen in amazement to the sounds that came from their home.

Flick had written to Jade of her adventures, when Flick had been backpacking down through France and had met Sasha and the two had hit it off straight away, working their way across France, wine picking, bar work. Whatever they could to earn money to carry on exploring. As Jade was driving her battered VW van, she remembered how envious she was all those years ago of the freedom and lifestyle. Well, now she was making her way to join them. When Flick set off, Jade had just gone to Uni, as her parents wanted. Five years to be a lawyer. She had loved uni life, but so longed to travel and the letters had kept coming. She knew what she wanted to do. So with a degree under her belt and with Dora, her faithful battered VW, packed with everything she needed, had set off with excitement and trepidation.

Rosie and Zac had been wandering around Asia for the last five years and had seen some of the most amazing places. Rosie knew that Zac was looking for one particular place for some reason that they never spoke about. Rosie had this feeling that what they were looking for would bring out the real reason for the search and something more important, at the back of her mind, kept flitting in and out and she could never quite grasp what it was. Rosie had not lost all of her knowledge and consciousness but in a lesser degree than Zac. What she knew was that she and Zac had this deep bond that went far deeper than the sexual relationship they shared. She felt in her bones that she had known Zac for eons, but still, it seemed a sort of slow unfoldment, a small snippet, that gave her some insight into events that were not always of this world. Zac was so frustrating when she spoke of it all. He would say it will come and this drove her always a little mad. Rosie knew she had to be the one in control and logical, but what for? Meanwhile, they were both in North India, in sight of the mountains they both loved. They were staying at this Ashram where everyone was expected to work to help run the place. No money charged. Working in the mornings and then the rest of the day for whatever was their desire. Sometimes meditation, sometimes listening to others and their stories or even a day out exploring the area. The whole place was so relaxed and peaceful. The visitors that came and went, so interesting, but just passing through. Rosie now knew this is where they would stay and felt in herself that this was a waiting time. But, what for? Zac would say, 'It will come'. How annoying.

Now, came a period of training and unfoldment. The Guru Xong who ran the place was elderly and becoming frail. It was obvious to Rosie that he saw in Zac the person who he wanted to take over from him when the time came. He was a wonderful man, full of the Ancient Wisdom. He began to teach Rosie and lead her slowly along the pathway. Slowly, as she learned, her memories of past lives and existence in other zones became clear. Xong never pushed her, letting her development happen at a pace she could cope with. The emergence of who she really, was the big shock and took her some time to accept and come to terms. Zac had gone off on his own up into the mountains to be alone. Preparing himself with what was to come. He had enjoyed his time with Rosie, and in some ways, reluctant for it to end, but he knew the time had come for their purpose for being on this planet to begin. It would alter everything. He had taken over a body of an eight-year-old, with his full consent on another level. Consequently, he had not lost all of his knowledge or consciousness.

Now he needed this time alone to bring forth the rest of his knowledge and full consciousness of who he was. To finetune his communication with the Elders on higher levels, especially Mosstle. He knew Rosie was in good hands with Xong, who was training her in the disciplines and so bringing her to acknowledge who she was and her purpose of being here. It would change her totally, but Zac needed her logical aspect to help herself and him with the others to get through what was ordained.

Flick had been at the Ashram for some time now and was totally fascinated by Zac and Rosie. For some reason, she felt so drawn to them, feeling they were all the same.

Whatever that meant, she didn't know, just felt that she was to be part of whatever was to come. How confusing and mad did that sound? Flick had been accepted by Xong and he had been teaching her attention and concentration with meditation. Xong said, "Westerners lacked such disciplines in their lives."

Flick took her time with all she had learnt. Thinking she had loads of time, but then with the deterioration in Xong's health, she had become more diligent and also had taken on the role of caring.

Making sure Xong rested and ate as often as he should. Now Rosie also was helping with the care of Xong. Glad for her help in the care, Flick was pleased with that, but not so pleased that Xong was sharing his precious teaching time with Rosie.

Flick had written to Jade about Xong and all his teachings. How wonderful it all was, but very demanding. Flick had been saying how hard the self-discipline had been to put into action and how she wished that Jade could come before it was too late. Flick had no idea that Jade was already driving her battered VW Dora through Europe to join Flick in India. She was yet to also tell Jade about Zac and Rosie. She didn't know why but wanted to keep that to herself for the time being.

Flick had also had a letter from Sasha saying she was on her way to join Flick. Sasha had fallen for a young man who ran a hostel in the mountains of the Himalayas when Flick and her had stayed at the hostel. Four years down the line it was all over, so now Sasha was on her way. Flick pondered about this, seemed that there must be a special reason that at this time everything had happened to bring her to the Ashram.

Jade had been enjoying her travels through Europe, taking her time, thinking with a smile on her face, how surprised Flick will be when she arrived. It was Flick's last letter that made her decide to leave now. Suddenly, after reading all about Flick's training with Xong, she felt she had to go now. Now, she suddenly felt an urgent need to get there as soon as possible. She had written a letter to her saying she was on her way, but it never got posted. Still nestling in her handbag. *Well,* she thought to herself, she will push on as fast as Dora would let her. As long as she got there it wouldn't matter if Dora gave up then. She just had to get there, that was all that mattered.

Sasha stopped at the gates of the Ashram, she was so tired but so glad to there. She looked at the gates and through them could see the mountains framed in the distance.

Picking up her rucksack, her step lightened, she walked through the gates, it felt like coming home. Flick was in the garden working in the vegetable patch looked up and saw Sasha. Dropping her trowel ran down the path to hug Sasha with such vigour, at the same time jumping up and down with the joy of seeing each other again.

"Oh, I am so glad you are here."

"Any tea going?" Laughed Sasha. They started up the path leading to the first building.

"Still the same Sasha, always wanting tea. Come and meet everyone."

At that very moment, Jade was only a day away and Zac was on his way back.

Knowing that everyone will be there by the time he returned. It was time.

Sasha felt instantly at home as she sat and chatted with Rosie and Flick. Xong was relaxing and listening to the girls talk. He felt strangely relieved, for at last, it was all coming together, and when Zac returned he knew his part had been done. He could, at last, take a back seat. He knew his time to leave this planet was almost here. He sat and felt the powerful forces building up. The girls were talking about Jade, Flick saying how she wished her friend was here with them all.

Xong smiled to himself, he knew she was on the way. He could feel the energies pulling her here and could sense her energy and excitement as she came closer. He sat and tuned in on her, putting a protecting ring around her as she hastened towards her destiny. Then he drifted into a deeper meditation, tuning in with the elders to absorb as much as he could of the info and energy of what was to be. Then he drifted into the healing hall absorbing the rays for maintenance for his physical body.

Jade pulled the hand brake on firmly, as Dora juddered to a stop. She was here, she couldn't believe it. Glancing up the drive and beyond at the mountains, the tears suddenly burst forth, relief, trepidation, a little fear, a mixture of happiness, tiredness and excitement. Such mixed emotions shook her body and mind. A tap on the van window and there stood a little old man with understanding in his eyes holding out his hand to her. Jade opened up the van door and half fell into the old man's arms.

"You are here now and safe."

Xong and Jade both looked at each other and then up at the mountains.

"Zac will be here in a day or two. Enough time for you to recover. Come with me now."

"Breathe in slowly through the nose, hold, now breathe slowly out through your mouth. That's it, again. Breathe in, hold, breathe out. Now as your body relaxes with the breath, just let go of all tension, problems, worldly things. Be still within. Be one with all."

Xong was taking the girls through their daily meditation, each day taking them deeper, closer to their true selves, helping them to expand their consciousness. Bringing them every day nearer to the point of recognition of who they truly were. Xong was amazed at the speed the girls progressed. For years he had taken these classes with those that came and went. Just a few decided to stay, to live this life. But in his experience, never had he met such as these girls. He knew they had roles to play and he was playing his part in what was to come. They were all just waiting for Zac.

Rosie who had remembered lives where she had searched for young girls to become pupils of the Master, now recognised who Zac really was and the essential part Flick, Jade and Sasha had been in those lives. Zac was later than expected and Rosie was a little concerned.

She laughingly said to the others, "In many lifetimes I have looked, searched and been there for you girls, but never have I had to go and search for Zac. Really must go and search for him."

All three girls stood and said in unison, "We will come with you."

"One of you must stay with Xong. I think that should be you, Jade, mainly because you have been rather tired since you arrived," stated Rosie with the firmness required of her new role.

"We will give Zac one more night and leave in the morning for the mountains."

Xong nodded in agreement.

The next morning, Rosie was up early and on her way to wake Flick and Sasha. Nearly jumped out of her skin when a deep voice said, "Morning Rosie."

There stood Zac, dusty, tired looking, but so different. She went to throw herself into his arms, "Oh, thank goodness."

But she stopped mid-throw. He was different, he looked like Zac but she knew he was so changed. For a few moments, she was in awe until Zac said, "I could do with a hug, Rosie."

That broke the impasse and she threw herself tearfully into his open arms.

"I know that I have changed, you have changed too, Rosie. Everything now will be as it should be. We have had some good times together and I will treasure those always and you must too as well. What is to come will be hard for all of us to adjust."

Zac tenderly kissed Rosie saying, "I need a bath, food, then I need to sleep."

It was 48 hours later that Zac finally woke up.

After food and a walk in the fresh air, Zac first went into a confab with Xong.

Requiring from Xong his thoughts and feelings of the progress of the girls. Xong detailed what he saw in each of the four.

"Rosie, well, she is seeing who she is and coming to terms with her role to come. Also seeing her relationship to all, and even in the last few days, coming to terms about the Elders and her discovery of Mosstle, her soul mate. This is such a

131

huge transition for her, but her ascending logic is helping her through."

Zac was very quiet for a few moments.

"Rosie has been on loan to me from Mosstle for many lifetimes. This must have been such a huge revelation. I am glad you think she has held her own. I am so thankful to you too."

Xong nodded and carried on, "Flick, well, she has been with me for many years, she has been just happy to carry on every day, learning at her own pace. Never been driven to find more, until she met you and Rosie. Then she woke up and started delving deeper, was horrified at the strength of her emotions and has been struggling badly since other lifetimes have become clear."

Zac looked at Xong and said, "And Sasha."

"Not a long time with Sasha, but she has the ability to calmly accept most things that happen, as quite normal. She has this thing about her that she really already knows and it just being confirmed."

"Now to Jade." Added Zac.

"Well, Jade flew in like a banshee and straight into everything as if she has been here all her life. I think her lifelong friendship with Flick and all the letters exchanged, made it all so familiar. Her instructions from me have made her realise that there is so much more to come. I believe her stoicism will pull her through."

"Thank you, Xong. You have certainly made my task easier."

The two sat in still compatible silence watching the evening close. The sun fading over the mountains.

"Jade has always loved this time of day," said a reflective Zac.

Zac sat facing the girls cross-legged on a pile of cushions. As he sat like this, he was temporarily transported to another time and place, long ago, when they all had last sat like this, in perfect harmony with one another. Zac pondered upon how long would this harmony between the girls would last when they knew what was to come.

Well! he thought to himself. *Hopefully they had at last, learned to control and use their emotions, given that they will have almost complete consciousness when they start.*

He reflected that it was an excellent idea of Mosstles, that Jade and Flick especially should know each other well before it all kicked off. Well, it has to work this time. He looked at the girls loving each one with depth and said, "Well, I want you to listen to what I have to say. No interruptions please, just be patient and digest."

Zac moved more comfortably on his cushion and took a deep breath.

"Long before time, when we were all atoms. I vibrated and you were all pulled towards me because you are on the same pattern. We set off on a cosmic journey, gathering a few more atoms on the way of some similarity in vibration. Well, we all began some form of life in another universe, far from this one, but mistakes were made and the universe collapsed into itself. We escaped and retreated to another level.

"Where it was pondered upon, probed and examined for the reasons why. It was found that it was the uncontrolled emotions of all that created negativity that became strong enough to create destruction."

Zac paused a moment, drank deeply out of glass, looked at his girls and saw what each one was remembering. He gave them a moment or two to balance their own emotional reaction. He noted Rosie was balancing this with logic. *Good*, he thought he needed her strong logically approach. Zac went on to explain that it was decided to come to this universe as they couldn't afford another collapse and it had been noted that negative energy was already gaining ascendancy and the main overriding energy of this universe is love and compassion. So as he, Zac, Lord of Tantra, was decided to bring this way of control to the planet earth. So many thousands of years ago, they all started lifetimes like humans with very limited conciseness. Rosie was his logic balance with Sasha assisting balancing, Flick and Jade, who were his two ladies in nearly every life, but each life failed because of raw uncontrolled emotion, leading to Flick and Jade always killing each other one way or another. So more consciousness was accelerated and a new law passed that if one of the girls was killed the other was put to death. So, in theory, this made the two of them guard each other.

Flick and Jade looked at each other with dismay. Realising the heavy responsibility of the situation. Zac paused again giving the girls time. Flick went to say something and Zac raised his hand.

"Not yet. This is now earth's last chance. You must learn to work with each other without jealously and envy, turning the negative energy through tantra to positive spiritual energy. We might just be able to manage to turn this around and this universe will be saved. It is fast running out of time and if we change a massive lot of energy around, it will start to affect everything."

Zac knew he had to lead his three girls down this path slowly at first. He planned to take each of them, away for a week at a time. Somewhere quiet, away from everything else, to build personal relationships. In other lives, Flick always wanted to be first and would fight Jade to be so, Sasha never worried were and when except in one particular lifetime. So in this instance, he would take Sasha first and then Jade, leaving Flick to last. This would be the first real test.

He informed Xong and he in return told Zac about a hut that the Ashram owned some miles away. Quite isolated. Zac told the girls and Rosie's first job was to help balance the two that were left behind.

Early the next morning, Zac and Sasha set off on their hike to the hut where they going to spend a week alone. Sasha strode along as if it was the most natural thing in the world to be going off for what was the beginning of events that would totally change all their lives. Zac privately wondered if she really understood what she was to take part in.

These three events to come would probably be the only times each of the girls will be alone with Zac. When the real works comes, it would be very different.

Life back at the Ashram went on as usual except one big difference, that is a totally different Rosie, was very much in charge. Flick and Jade wondered from time to time about what was happening up at the Ashrams hut, but mainly because they didn't know; apart from pondering, it didn't seem to bother either of them. Their lifelong friendship deepened. Xong watched and continued with their development classes, and saw and understood the wisdom of Zac taking Sasha first.

It was a very vibrant Sasha that returned with Zac. She just glowed and couldn't take her eyes off Zac. Flick had felt a strange sensation flood her body and felt an odd rage that took her by surprise. Pushing it down she stepped up and warmly welcomed her friend back. Jade felt a strange sensation as well, hers was more of a filling up of energy that reminded her of Zac. Raising her eyes to meet his, felt this energy flood even more in her whole being.

"Be ready to leave in the morning, Jade."

Zac moved off, leaving Jade feeling confused and a little faint.

Zac led Jade very gently to the bed in the hut. Jade viewed the bed with the thought in her mind that this was where it happened with Sasha.

It was as if he read her mind.

"No, it was not here."

And Zac sat down and patted the side of the bed. Jade carefully sat down.

"This is silly. I don't know why I am so nervous. I love you deeply and can now remember some of our other lives." She looked longingly into Zac's eyes and fell deeply into their depths.

"Whatever is now going to happen, I want you to remember that the love I have for you is yours and yours alone. Same as my love for Flick and Sasha is theirs and theirs alone. Neither one detracts from the other."

"I remember you saying that to me many lifetimes ago, I think we were birdlike then."

Jade pondered, slowly remembering. She took Zac's hands kissed each of them and then reached up to his lips gently nibbled his lips and Zac grabbed her, kissing, bruising her lips, pulled roughly as Jade fell on the bed.

"I was going to take you with care, but I need to join with you now." Pushing her legs urgently open, thrust into her with a gasp of relief then with delight and need.

"At last."

Jade needed no further prompting.

After the urgency was spent, Zac removed the rest of her clothes and began to explore her body. Tenderly tracing the outlines of her face, butterfly moves down her neck, leading down to her breasts, Zac examined them with delight, fingering the nipples that stood to attention.

"I remember a lifetime when you lost your nipples in battle, glad to say I doubt that will happen in this lifetime." He lapped around each nipple then stretched them with his teeth. Jade gasped and made to grab him.

"No, not now. I just want you to relax here, while I get to know your body well."

He stroked his way to her navel, tracing around it and passing on to gently massage her thighs, stroking upwards with a glancing and flicking action on her sex, sending Jade nearly frantic for him.

"Good," was all Zac said.

He sat cross-legged between her legs, raising them onto his. Spread her wide, opening her lower lips, drew his fingers around, getting closer and closer to her sex bud. When he touched it, first with his fingers, then with his tongue, she went wild bucking till spasms of climaxes hit her body.

Zac held her and waited until she was calmer.

"I think that is enough for today, rest now."

With that said, Zac rose, tucked the covers around Jade and left her to rest.

The week passed with such speed. Jade knew every inch of Zac's body and Zac knew hers, every part, each reaction, her mind and her true self, which was fast unfolding past lives and her roles in the intimate relationship with Zac and the others in the group. She now was fully aware of the trouble on this level that she and Flick had caused with jealousy and how it harmed everything. Jade was contrite but determined that this time there could be no failure.

Whatever emotions she felt must be understood and then controlled, eventually having no affect upon her at all.

Well, she thought as she packed her backpack, *the first test will come when Zac takes Flick for her week.*

Flick and Zac left early and Jade watched them walking down the path, holding hands, she felt a tinge in her gut. But thought of the words Zac had spoken, recognising the feeling and put it to one side.

"This time we all have to make it," she said to the room.

Turning, to get on with the day, she walked fast and collided with Sahsa.

"Came to see how you are," Sasha said and gave Jade a big hug.

"Let's get on with Xong's breakfast."

Zac led the way up the steep path to the hut with an eagerness that he could hardly contain. All the energies that had been let loose with Sasha and Jade swirled around him. He stopped a moment to control these, pushing them through, out of his crown to be used for the good of the universe. Feeling in control again, muttered under his breath.

"Should have done that sooner."

He had to be so in control, how could he expect his girls to be in control if he wasn't himself. This was of utmost importance.

They lay in bed sated. *That was something else,* thought Zac. He thought over his three girls and the way it was for each of them. Flick and Jade so alike. Energies so fierce. He thought over the many lives with them. Always planning ways to get rid of the other. He needed both for this to work. Sighing, it just has to be right this time.

With now his full consciousness and the girls rapidly down this pathway, *Surely,* he thought.

Turning to Flick, he felt himself go hard again; he rolled her over on her stomach and was deep in her before she was barely awake.

Chapter 17

The Elders were sitting and had called Zac/Zude up for the meeting, it was unknown to call for someone midlife. Mosstle was called and informed that Zude would be here shortly. Leaving his physical body in a meditative trance was sometimes dangerous, as the thread could be broken and the lifetime lost.

Zac was laying on his bed; he had left instructions that no one was to disturb him under any circumstance. The girls had decided to take turns sitting outside his room, making sure no one went near him. It was Jade who sat there now, reading some old book Xong had instructed that all the girls should read. It was on trance and astral travel and the other different levels that can be reached with practise.

Zac's breath became deeper, then as he left his body his breathing became more shallow and calmer. His true self came through as he left his personality behind. He appeared as his true self in the ring and there was Mosstle waiting for him.

"Do you know what this is all about?" He asked of Mosstle. Mosstle wrapped his arms around his friend, steadying him as he stepped from the ring.

"No, but I have an idea."

After a few moments, the two friends walked off in the direction of the Hall of the Root Energy. There Zude acclimatised himself, greeting friends and taking pleasure from the Hall's energies.

"Better," said Mosstle, as they both sat by a fountain that spilt out purple and violet hues, infusing them both with the balancing rays.

Then they both thought themselves to the council chamber where they found all the Elders and the Wise One waiting.

"Welcome and peace be with you both, come sit here." The Wise One was infused with white white light, filling the Chamber with his aura.

Mosstle and Zude bowed with deep respect.

"We want to know from you, Zude, if you think that Flute and Jacelet are fully prepared, and are you sure they are going to make it work this time?

"They must control the energies and tip the balance to positive. You must have no doubt in your mind. It is imperative that we know for sure.

"Another universe has been primed and ready for upgrading and if you have any doubt in your mind we will pull the plug on the earth universe before it is destroyed by its occupants and then concentrate on the next."

Zude looked straight at the Wise One. A few moments where thoughts and feelings passed between them.

"My girls are different this time, the care taken for Jade and Flick to know each other well, before it all started has made a big difference. I am confident."

A buzz rang through the Elders, their thoughts whirling round the Wise One, who absorbed and instantly knew.

"Let it be, but be warned, any relapse we will instantly pull the plug."

It was Rosie who was sitting outside the door when Zac was making his way back into the physical. Rosie heard a sound, a low gasp and she entered the room quickly but quietly. She sat next to the bed watching Zac. His colour was not good and she realised that the strain of him being away from his body for such a long time had made it difficult for him to return with ease. She held his hand and concentrated on pulling him back to his body. Zac convulsed a little and this too was worrying as he always had such command and control. She concentrated and slowly the colour flooded back and his breathing became normal. Zac struggled to speak.

"Gosh, that was hard, the cord almost broke."

Rosie stroked his brow.

"You frightened me."

"Don't tell the girls; keep this between us, Rosie."

They sat together in silence as his strength returned.

"Sorry for scaring you."

"What did the elders want?"

Zac then related all that had passed and said, "Mosstle sends his love to you and told me I had to take great care of you or else!"

Zac laughed quietly.

It was sometime later that the two of them left Zac's room to find some food and drink. It was late and the others were all asleep, which Zac was grateful for as he didn't want his girls seeing him like this.

They were sitting over coffee while Zac related all about his encounter with the Elders. The girls were quiet, horrified that so much hung on how they managed this next stage of this life.

Zac spoke saying how he and Rosie had spoken well into the night on how to go about this next phase. He asked the girls if they remembered anything of a life where they all took part in the tantric arts.

Jade nodded and said, "I remember I had my throat cut."

Zac laughed, "Well, nothing like that will happen but it is serious that you work with me. And it might at first feel strange in this day and age, but you have all spent time with me and know some of the moves and it will become the norm to you all as you remember much more.

"We will move into the upper building which will become private to us and no one else will enter. Xong will take care of all in the lower building with the other older residents caring for him and helping him in any way. The ashram will run as it always has and no one will know what is happening with us all."

It had all began with a bang, straight in with the rituals. Rosie stood close by watching and balancing with her and Mosstle's form of logic. She related to him on the higher level, so her logic would be stronger.

Stark naked, Zac first took Flick, with Jade and Sasha standing on each side with one hand on Zac's shoulder and one on Flick's. They rotated places as Zac took the other two girls by turn. Their combined energies whirled and travelled through their bodies with Rosie directing them out for balancing with the other world energies. Zac performed over and over again, the girls changing places until a point came where they all could no more.

Exhausted, they fell into a heap. Zac went and sat with Rosie studying the energies and colours that flowed around.

"Well, Rosie, I am well pleased with the result, no negative vibes from the girls and look at what we have created. It has all begun. Tomorrow we will expand the energies with just Flick and Jade."

Rosie and Zac sat in a comfortable silence while the girls slept.

They lay in a triangle shape. Zac's mouth on Flick's sex bud, Jade attending to Zac's sex and Flick stimulating Jade's sex. The energies and power was huge; the girls coming over and over again. Becoming very vocal, Zac took a moment to say, "Keep going, even when it gets painful. These energies are great and the universe will certainly react to these."

Because of the strength of the energies, Rosie sat outside the door, with Sasha helping. Concentrating on the three for the strength to carry on.

Several hours later, the trio could no longer maintain their efforts. Sore and exhausted, they just fell into a stupor and slept where they lay, in the triangle shape. The energies carried on working, swirling around purple, gold and silver, increased vibration from the root energy they all started with.

Zac was deep in thought, he was experiencing some weakness in his body, he was most surprised and puzzled. Never had his control and stamina been a problem. They all had so much to learn and expand the tantric ways, to transform the negative energy that abound this planet.

He knew that the balance had begun to show some change and with this change, it should soon start to show in people's behaviour. It was so important to keep on going strong. Flick and Jade who took on most of the tantric practises, although

144

exhausted at times, were doing such an excellent job with their personal emotions in harmony with each other, which had been, in so many other lives, the cause of many premature life endings.

Zac was so proud of them both and if possible, loved them more for their dedication to getting it right.

Zac was taking Jade for a way they had not attempted for many lifetimes and he was not sure how she would react. He was stepping up the tantra, increasing the strength of the energies. They had all been briefed beforehand. While he attended to Jade, the others were needed to stand close, to have contact with the energies which will be of an increased strength. Rosie, holding Jade's head, using her logic, with Flick and Sasha holding each of Jade's hands.

Zac stood between Jade's legs with a small whip and was teasing Jades sex with light glancing flicks, spreading around the area and back on to her sex. Jade was nearly beside herself with the energy created and the constant climaxes. The energy flooded through Flick and Sasha through their hands and they too were vibrating with constant powerful climaxes.

Rosie, with her logic control, watched the energies and when they all blended together in a new powerful force and as it reached a powerful dangerous destructive point she called out 'stop'. She had been watching well and had been so glad to stop these proceedings, but it had to be at the right point.

After this, the new energy force created certainly made new inroads into their activities as all of them had this new energy flowing throughout their bodies and other levels. Zac then took his girls in every way possible.

Jade, taking a moment to herself, thought laughingly that there was just no space or time to be envious or jealous and, how petty all these emotions were. The work was so full-on and hard that they were constantly exhausted. Zac seemed driven. He was in a hurry as he had realised he was failing. The time he had been called to the elders meeting had indeed damaged his cord and he was very aware that his time on this planet was now limited. He had to train his girls in all methods so that they could carry on without him on this level. He knew that with this new energy he could control all from another level. So he pushed his girls hard.

He spoke of this to only to Xong. Zac needed him to stay on this planet for as long as possible.

Months past, the girls hardly noticed the change of the seasons with all that was constantly going on. Zac teaching them to create energy forces with each other and still taking his girls as much as he could. He wanted them to know how much he loved them and how proud he was of their progress in all directions.

When it happened, it was very shocking and sudden. Zac had just been going through their lessons of pleasuring each other and he had taken each of his girls after. Stood to take a drink and just dropped.

Chapter 18

Zac had been gone now, three months, and the girls were still in shock. Xong had explained how his cord had weakened and that was the reason he had been teaching the girls to be able to work without him. Jade felt as though a part of her was missing.

She made frequent visits to the hut where it had all kicked off. They had all scattered his ashes nearby, in sight of the mountains they all loved so much. Jade knew the work had to go on, with their transformation of energies, they had been making a great difference to the balance of this planet. You could feel the difference, in the air.

Energies so strong but had the strength to start lightening the people and there was less mass crowd destruction and this was a major leap forward. Jade was amazed that what they did changed everything so much for the humans. She remembered so well her lives as a bird-like creature and of the shock of that world sliding into negative destruction. She knew that she and Flick must get their act together again very soon.

Sasha had been saying that for days now. Rosie knew of Zac's failing health, but still, it had hit her so hard. She knew he was all right, back with Mosstle and the others.

She was waiting with impatience for them to get going again and that was why she was walking up to the hut to find Jade. She knew she had to take charge and get it all going again. It was so urgent. She hoped to find Flick, she hadn't seen her for days.

Rosie and Jade sat looking at the mountains. They had talked for most of the day. Each talking of memories of lives past. Their most precious moments they had experienced with Zac they shared with each other. It was a kind of healing and Jade felt closer to him realising he was part of her and that part would never diminish.

Evening was falling fast and those moments of failing light and long shadows closed around them both, bonding them fast when a voice broke the silence.

"Flick, at last, thank goodness, been so worried."

Rosie moved to hug the girl and Jade followed suit. The three stood in emotional silence, their arms around each other.

Slowly Flick started to sob, with her shoulders shaking, finally, her legs gave way.

The three of them sunk to the ground, tears following from all, holding each other as slowly the storm abated. Then, slowly standing, walked inside the hut that was so full of good memories. They spent the night laying close together, feeling the presence of Zac with them, and slowly, at last, the healing began.

The next morning, they set off. Back to the Ashram, finding Sasha bustling around Xong, who, looking pale was having one of his not so good days. *We can't lose him as well,* was Rosie's immediate thought.

They all sat down at the table having breakfast together. Sasha, relieved that everyone was back, was tinged a little by her concern about Xong. Xong, so pleased that the girls were all back together, sat with them feeling better by each passing moment. He knew in himself he had to hang onto life longer than expected. He was so sad at the loss of Zac, but feeling his presence strongly, knew that the work had to go on and it would, with the strength of Zac's essence. It was only his physical that was missing.

The next morning, the girls were back in their rooms at the back of the Ashram.

Rosie, checking on the girls, that they were all okay said, "You need to get to it, you know what to do. Today I will leave you and see how Xong is and sort out some sort of care rota with the others. We need him, so we have to take care of him."

Flick and Jade, feeling Zac's presence, lay down on the large bed disrobing each other.

Sasha slipped on the bed between the two, slowly sighed and opened herself up for their attention. Then they formed the triangle and got to work.

Jade was sitting in the garden enjoying the sunshine, just wondering where all the years had gone. Xong had lived on several more years and had died quietly just short of his 90th year. He had left a very capable lady to run the ashram and she ran the place with gusto, training all who came to learn deep meditation and those energies had blended well, with all of those that the girls made. The girls now just had to lie with each other, holding hands to be able to produce the same energies by mind. *A good thing*, thought Jade, for as they got a lot older, it would have become a problem to carry on the same way. It was a very sad Jade, who had been so shocked with the passing of Rosie. She had always been there to balance the energies. She missed her, but Rosie was with Mosstle now. Oh, how Jade missed Zac's physical presence. You would think after all these years it would have eased, but she was also so aware of his energies, that filled her being constantly and that was without a doubt the biggest comfort.

They had worked so hard after Zac had died, and Xong had said that it had made such a huge difference to planet earth. The energies they had created blended with the universal ones and had caused the negative ones that the earth was wallowing in to negate, and all they had done caused the planet to restore itself. Now the people had a chance, as long peace reigned in all nations – the whole race was progressing. Jade could hardly believe that what they had done could make such a huge difference.

Jade watched the sun going down, her favourite time. Dusk was settling with a sudden coolness in the air. She stood up carefully to go inside.

It was her turn to sit with Flick, who slept nearly all the time now and was fading slowly. Sasha had been with her all afternoon and now it was Jade's turn.

Now, it was Flick's turn to leave. It was like she was burnt out and Jade herself had to admit she felt worn out herself. She was aware that her life force was not so strong.

They never spoke of it, but Jade thought that Sasha knew they were all not so strong.

She had felt a slight twinge of envy that Flick would be back with Zac first. Jade laughed to herself as she walked towards the Ashram. But not for long, Flick would only be there a short while before she herself would join them.

The Old Law through many lifetimes.

When one of them dies, the other has to die as well.

The End or is it the Real Beginning.